The cemetery was one of the oldest in southern California. It was simple and beautiful, with wild flowers springing up between tombstones. Glossy ivy leaves carpeted the gray walls of the church, and a large willow tree swayed gracefully in the breeze.

The mourners assembled around the open grave as Nick's casket was tenderly laid to rest. Jessica, his parents, and his closest friends— Elizabeth included—were given dark red roses to toss onto the casket before the plot was covered with earth.

Suddenly Elizabeth realized it was her turn. She walked past the grave diggers, her eyes nearly blinded by tears, and looked down at Nick's final resting place. Elizabeth uttered a silent prayer and tossed her rose until it landed, six feet down, with the others.

As she left to take her place by Jessica's side, Mr. Fox picked up a shovel and tossed in the first clump of earth. The dirt and pebbles made a harsh sound as they struck the coffin.

Elizabeth wanted to cover her ears to block out the noise. How could something as simple as a little earth hitting a wooden box sound so ugly? Why did it have to sound so final? And how could Jessica stand to hear it without breaking down?

Bantam Books in the Sweet Valley University series.
Ask your bookseller for the books you have missed.

And don't miss these Sweet Valley
University Thriller Editions:

Visit the Official Sweet Valley Web Site on the Internet at:

http://www.sweetvalley.com

SWEET VALLEY UNIVERSITY®

Don't Let Go

Written by
Laurie John

Created by
FRANCINE PASCAL

BANTAM BOOKS
NEW YORK • TORONTO • LONDON • SYDNEY • AUCKLAND

RL 8, age 14 and up

DON'T LET GO

A Bantam Book / March 1999

Sweet Valley High® and Sweet Valley University®
are registered trademarks of Francine Pascal.
Conceived by Francine Pascal.

 Produced by 17th Street Productions,
a division of Daniel Weiss Associates, Inc.
33 West 17th Street
New York, NY 10011.

ISBN: 0-553-49265-9

Published simultaneously in the United States and Canada

Bantam Books are published by Bantam Books, a division of Random
House, Inc. Its trademark, consisting of the words "Bantam Books" and
the portrayal of a rooster, is Registered in U.S. Patent and Trademark
Office and in other countries. Marca Registrada. Bantam Books, 1540
Broadway, New York, New York 10036.

PRINTED IN THE UNITED STATES OF AMERICA

OPM   0 9 8 7 6 5 4 3 2 1

To Erica Stone

Chapter One

Sunlight streamed through stained-glass windows and made exquisite patterns on the cool, marble floor. The gentle strains of a string quartet floated through the vestry. Giant vases of lilies had been placed beside each pew. The air inside the chapel was fresh and cool. A butterfly flew in through the open doors and fluttered up toward the rafters.

Jessica Wakefield sat regally in the front pew. She looked beautiful but pale. Her porcelain complexion contrasted dramatically with her severe black dress. Her posture was ramrod straight. She stared ahead unblinkingly, as if she were oblivious to the sobs and groans surrounding her as she listened to the funeral oration honoring the too-brief life of her boyfriend, Nick Fox.

The chapel was packed to capacity. Chief Ernest Wallace, Detectives Dub Harrison and Bill

1

Fagen, Officer Graham Stevens, and the entire Sweet Valley precinct filled the pews to overflowing. Lila Fowler, Denise Waters, and Alexandra Rollins stood respectfully with the rest of Jessica's sorority sisters at the back of the church, among countless other faces familiar from the campus of Sweet Valley University. Older people whom Jessica didn't recognize were crowded against the walls, openly weeping.

They weren't the only ones. Tears streamed down Chief Wallace's weather-beaten cheeks. Dub swiped at his eyes with the back of his hand, while Lila Fowler dabbed at hers with a Belgian-lace handkerchief. Jessica was dimly aware that the women sitting on either side of her—her twin sister, Elizabeth, and Nick's mother, Rhoda Fox—were crying. *Everyone* was crying. Everyone except Jessica. Throughout the whole of that packed congregation, her eyes alone remained dry.

Jessica idly counted the candles on either side of the altar. She flicked a piece of lint from the deep black crepe of her long skirt. She traced the gold lettering on the cover of her prayer book. She stared at the American flag that had been draped over Nick's casket. It annoyed her that one of the corners, the one on the right, was curling upward, as if the flag hadn't been ironed out properly.

She knew that people must be wondering why she wasn't more openly upset; she could feel their questioning gazes upon her. But Jessica was beyond tears.

Don't they understand? she wondered miserably. *Don't they realize I've dried up inside?*

After a moment of silence Chief Wallace was called up to deliver his eulogy. He made his way slowly toward the podium, his shoulders hunched, his steps heavy.

Jessica jumped slightly as Elizabeth took her hand. Jessica squeezed her sister's hand in return, but for once Elizabeth's touch failed to comfort her. Even Elizabeth couldn't understand how she was feeling. Elizabeth, who had been able to read Jessica's every mood for the past eighteen years, seemed light-years away from her now. How could Elizabeth possibly understand what it felt like to lose Nick?

Jessica turned to look at Nick's parents. Normally the Foxes were a distinguished-looking couple, but today the only remarkable thing about them was the pain etched in grim lines upon their faces.

Impulsively Jessica grasped the sleeve of Mrs. Fox's black suit jacket. Mrs. Fox turned in surprise, but her expression softened slightly at the sight of Jessica's pale face.

"Mrs. Fox, I can't understand what it must feel like to lose your only son," Jessica whispered hoarsely. "But you have to know how much I loved Nick . . . how much I share your pain. . . ." Jessica trailed off, unable to continue.

"I know how much you loved each other," Mrs. Fox replied. "It meant so much to Ben and me to see Nicky so happy." She gave Jessica a watery smile. "Nicky dated a lot of girls over the years, but it was obvious that you were his true love."

Jessica nodded silently, her chest tightening.

"You were perfect for each other," Nick's father, Ben Fox, joined in. His hand shook slightly as he reached around his wife to give Jessica's shoulder a soothing pat. "You're so feisty and independent, so adventurous. Just like Nicky was."

"He was so proud of how brave you were," Mrs. Fox concurred. "So proud. He was impressed by your determination to join the force."

"He'd get so furious with me every time I brought it up," Jessica protested with a small, bittersweet smile.

"That's only because he loved you so much," Mr. Fox said. "He was so protective of you. Deep down, he admired your fearlessness. He just never wanted you to be exposed to danger."

"He couldn't bear the thought of anything happening to you, Jessica. He would have given his life for you—" Mrs. Fox's voice cracked. She turned away from Jessica and sought the comfort of her husband's arms.

Jessica stiffened as if she had been slapped. She

4

knew Mrs. Fox had only meant to be kind, but her words hammered painfully at Jessica's conscience. Nick *had* given his life for her. If Nick hadn't testified in Jessica's place at Clay DiPalma's trial, he would still be alive. He wouldn't have been shot in cold blood on the witness stand. He wouldn't have died on a stretcher surrounded by strangers who had no chance of saving his life.

Do the Foxes know Nick took the stand to protect me? Jessica wondered guiltily. *Do they know this is all my fault?*

She glanced uneasily at the Foxes. Their faces were fragile and mournful, but Jessica could have sworn that for a moment, incrimination flashed in their eyes.

They know, she realized. *They must know. They blame me, and I blame myself. I blame myself.*

Jessica buried her face in her hands.

"Peppermint or chamomile?" Dana Upshaw brushed a lock of mahogany hair out of her eyes and held up two tea bags for inspection.

"Um, chamomile. With extra honey, please." Felicity Jones sniffled and wrapped her fuzzy blue bathrobe around her.

"Coming right up." Dana put on the kettle and bustled around the kitchen inside the off-campus house she shared with Felicity and three other women. She quickly assembled two delicate china

5

cups, a small plate of cookies, another of thinly sliced lemon, and a glass dish of honey on a painted wooden tray. With a flourish she placed a small bud vase in the middle of the tray and added a daisy she had picked from the front yard.

Felicity's eyebrows shot up as Dana padded over to the worn-out blue velour couch in her pajamas, balancing the tray precariously in front of her. "All this? *Pour moi?*" she asked in shock. "All right, Dana, spill."

"Spill? Spill what, the tea?" Dana joked, avoiding Felicity's gaze as she set the tray down on the battered cherry-wood coffee table.

"C'mon, Dana, what's with the Florence Nightingale act? I mean, it's not like I don't appreciate it, but it's hardly the Dana we've all come to know and love." Felicity reached for a gingersnap. "Is the psychology department conducting some kind of Stepford student experiment? I hope it pays well."

"Gee, thanks, Felicity. I didn't realize I was such a monster." Dana handed her housemate one of the rose-patterned cups.

"I didn't say you were," Felicity mumbled through a mouthful of cookie. "It's just that this is hardly your usual speed. Waking your roomies up at four A.M. practicing the third movement of a Haydn concerto, prancing around campus in an outfit guaranteed to make a monk drool—now

6

that's the Dana I know. But auditioning for Girl Scout of the Month? Didn't think that was in your nature."

Dana shrugged. "Just felt like it today, I guess."

"Why today?" Felicity reached for a tissue. "I'm willing to bet you and I are the only two SVU students *not* at that cop's funeral. I mean, the poor guy got killed for putting away a campus drug dealer. I'd be there if I didn't have a fever." She sneezed into the tissue for emphasis. "What's your excuse?"

Dana bent her head over her cup, hoping her hair would obscure the blush heating up her cheeks. Hmmm . . . what *was* her excuse anyway? That by showing up, she'd only cause the Wakefield twins more pain? That she'd run into Tom Watts, the last person on earth she wanted to see? That she happened to be the campus pariah right now?

"I just wanted to help you feel better," Dana began brightly. "I wanted to . . . um . . ." Dana raised her head and locked eyes with Felicity.

"Save it." Felicity held up a hand. "Look, I know there's no love lost between you and the Wakefields. But why avoid them now? This is the perfect opportunity to put the past behind you."

Dana sighed deeply. "*I* can forget about the past, but I don't see how anyone else can." She winced as the memory of Elizabeth's stricken face flashed before her eyes. "I feel like the whole

7

campus hates me right now. I mean, you should have tried being *me* last week. Everywhere I went, people acted like I had the Ebola virus. No one would sit with me in the cafeteria. No one would talk to me. Oh, sorry, my mistake. *Elizabeth* talked to me. What a disaster that was." Dana shook her head.

"Elizabeth talked to you?" Felicity wrapped her bathrobe more snugly around herself and shot Dana an inquisitive glance.

"If you can call it talking." Dana shuddered.

"Total catfight?"

"Not exactly." Dana sipped her tea. "Elizabeth was trying to be friendly. She was actually really sweet, but then she said something about how faithful Tom had been while they were split up."

"Faithful?" Felicity looked amused. "What did she think you and Tom had been doing all that time? Playing hopscotch?"

"Well, according to the Princess of Purity, Tom made out like we never did anything more than hold hands. You can imagine how good that made me feel." Dana laughed bitterly. "Anyway, I set the record straight."

"And?"

"And . . . let's just say, Elizabeth wouldn't be too thrilled to see me right now." Dana smirked. *That* was putting it mildly.

"You can't blame yourself," Felicity protested.

"Why was Elizabeth so naive? For that matter, why did *Tom* lie to her about how serious you guys were?"

"I think Tom just wants to forget the whole thing ever happened," Dana said quietly.

"Really?" Felicity looked shocked.

Dana shrugged. "Look, it's not the first time something like this has happened to me. Tom got what he wanted, and now he wants to pretend I don't exist."

"Jeez. So much for Tom Terrific," Felicity scoffed. "More like Tom Typical Male."

"Yeah. And to tell you the truth, I don't want to see Tom right now any more than he wants to see me."

Felicity reached over and rubbed Dana's shoulder. "I'm so sorry. I know how much Tom meant to you. I've gotta say you've been handling this really well, you know . . . considering."

"I suppose." Dana sat for a moment in silence. The truth was, deep down, she wasn't handling it well at all. She pasted a smile on her face. "So, Felicity, to answer your question, I believe my presence at Nick Fox's funeral would only make every last person there even more miserable than they already are."

"Hey, don't be so hard on yourself." Felicity scooted over on the couch, and Dana rested her head on her shoulder. "You just need to take some time for yourself right now. Put all this stuff behind you. Focus on your music, go shopping, forget about guys for a while. Maybe now that you're not wasting your time with that creep, you'll meet the love of your life."

"Maybe," Dana said, unconvinced.

Felicity gave Dana a consoling hug. "Look, I'd better get back to bed. Hang around me much longer and you'll start feeling a lot worse—believe me." Felicity stood up, grabbed her cough drops and tissues, and headed to her room.

"Feel better, Felicity," Dana called.

"You too, kiddo."

Dana took a sip of her chamomile tea and grimaced. Lukewarm. It tasted like weeds. Dana stomped over to the sink and unceremoniously dumped it down the drain. She needed to ingest *something*, but what?

She yanked open the refrigerator and began rummaging through old Chinese takeout boxes, half-eaten containers of yogurt, and cans of diet soda. Dana cautiously chose a newish-looking cup of strawberry yogurt but drew back in disgust when she opened the lid and discovered a thin film of green mold.

"Great." Dana tossed the container in the garbage. "Strawberries and *E. coli*. Just what the love doctor ordered."

Dana slammed the refrigerator shut in disgust

and caught sight of her reflection in the kitchen window. Her normally glossy mahogany curls hung limply down her back. Her glowing, tanned complexion had turned pale and wan, and her fiery hazel eyes had completely lost their sparkle.

She averted her gaze hastily, but not before the unpleasant image had burned itself in her mind. She glanced down at her baggy pajamas and sighed deeply. "Guaranteed to make a monk drool? I don't *think* so."

Dana squared her shoulders in determination. "OK. Enough of this noise," she declared. "No more baggy pajamas, and no more moldy yogurt! I'm taking myself to lunch, and I'm not going out looking like somebody's great-aunt Mildred either."

Dana spun on her heel and walked briskly toward her bedroom. It was about time she made herself beautiful again.

Is Jessica in shock? Elizabeth wondered. She shot her twin a questioning glance, but Jessica's face was partially obscured by her hair. She seemed completely unmoved by the eulogies and prayers being offered. Except for a brief moment when she had buried her face in her hands, her sister hadn't shown any emotion. Instead she sat perfectly still, as if she were carved from marble, not shedding a tear. Meanwhile Elizabeth was weeping enough for them both.

Maybe Jessica was in severe denial. For the past several days even Elizabeth had a hard time accepting Nick's death. She couldn't stop remembering how loving Nick had been toward Jessica, how perfectly they had complemented each other. They could have had an amazing future together. And now . . .

Phrases from Chief Wallace's eulogy floated through the air, echoing her own thoughts. "He was a young man of great promise and moral courage who risked his life in the name of justice. A young man who was cruelly cut down in his prime. A young man who still had so much love and life in him. . . ."

Elizabeth swallowed hard. It was all so unfair. She had been so sure that Jessica had finally met the right man. That at least one of them would be lucky in love.

She glanced over her shoulder toward where Tom Watts was standing and felt a twinge in her stomach. She couldn't help noticing how his dark suit and tie set off his good looks to perfection. He stood with his head bowed and his hands loosely clasped in front of him, his serious expression giving his face a mature dignity.

Was Tom thinking the same thing as she? How tragic it was for true love to end so brutally? Or was he distracting himself with memories of—

Stop it, Elizabeth told herself. Her cheeks

flamed. How could she have such petty and irrelevant feelings at a time like this?

Chief Wallace finished speaking, and the entire congregation stood as Nick's casket was carried out on the shoulders of eight strong pallbearers, all policemen from the Sweet Valley precinct.

Elizabeth filed out along with the rest of the mourners to the small cemetery that lay directly behind the church. She turned to take Jessica's arm but held back when she saw Mrs. Fox reach for her twin. It hurt Elizabeth not to be able to hold her sister, but she didn't want to come between Jessica and the Foxes. She knew that her sister's pain could hardly compare to the heartache Nick's parents were feeling.

The cemetery was one of the oldest in southern California. It was simple and beautiful, with wildflowers springing up between tombstones. Glossy ivy leaves carpeted the gray walls of the church, and a large willow tree swayed gracefully in the breeze.

The mourners assembled around the open grave as Nick's casket was tenderly laid to rest. Jessica, his parents, and his closest friends—Elizabeth included—were given dark red roses to toss onto the casket before the plot was covered with earth.

Mrs. Fox dropped the first rose. Her voice was barely audible as she mumbled a prayer. Elizabeth marveled at her sister's calm as she strode with great poise toward Nick's coffin and tossed her rose in with a graceful flick of her hand.

Suddenly Elizabeth realized it was her turn. She walked past the grave diggers, her eyes nearly blinded by tears, and looked down at Nick's final resting place. Elizabeth uttered a silent prayer and tossed her rose until it landed, six feet down, with the others.

As she left to take her place by Jessica's side, Mr. Fox picked up a shovel and tossed in the first clump of earth. The dirt and pebbles made a harsh sound as they struck the coffin.

Elizabeth wanted to cover her ears to block out the noise. How could something as simple as a little earth hitting a wooden box sound so ugly? Why did it have to sound so final? And how could Jessica stand to hear it without breaking down?

The grave diggers moved in to complete their job, and the mourners started filing away.

Thump. Thump. Thump.

Elizabeth began to feel restless. She had to leave, get far away from that horrible sound. "Jess? Do you think we should go now?" she asked gently.

Thump. Thump. Thump.

Jessica remained unmoved. She stared straight forward, eyes dry, face placid, watching the grave diggers pile dirt on Nick's coffin.

Thump. Thump. Thump.

Elizabeth couldn't stand it any longer. She felt as if she was about to faint. "Jess . . . I'll meet

14

you out front," she choked out before hurrying away. But as Elizabeth rushed past the mourners, one of her heels caught in the ground and twisted. She stumbled and nearly fell. A pair of strong hands steadied her.

Tom. Elizabeth gasped when she found herself looking into her ex-boyfriend's warm brown eyes. For a brief second she wanted to relax into Tom's arms. She wanted to feel his compassion, his support, to know that life and love still existed. Instead she pushed him angrily away.

"What?" Tom asked. "I was just trying to—"

"How dare you?" Elizabeth snarled.

"Liz, calm down, OK? Look . . . I know you're going through a lot right now."

"*Exactly.* So why not try showing me a little respect for once. I mean, this is not the time or the place to try and—and—"

"And help you? That's all I was doing. Honest. You looked like you were passing out." Tom took a step forward and extended his hand, but Elizabeth slapped it away. "Hey, stop it," Tom said gently. "You're starting to scare me."

"Why? Because I know what you're up to?"

"*What* are you *talking* about?"

"You're trying to take advantage of me right now, that's what," Elizabeth accused. "You were thinking, 'Gee, when would be the perfect time to convince Elizabeth that I'm actually a great, noble, decent guy? Hey, why not Nick Fox's funeral? She'll be so vulnerable, I bet I could sucker her into believing just about *anything.*'"

"Please, I know you don't really mean that," Tom said quietly. "God. You look so unhappy right now. You're breaking my heart, Liz."

"Well, I guess that makes us even," Elizabeth snapped. "Good-bye, Tom. And I *really mean that.*"

Todd dribbled the ball for a few seconds before he jogged to the center of the basketball court and let it fly. All net. "Not bad. Not bad at all," he muttered. Too bad there wasn't anyone around to see him sink one from beyond three-point range.

He wiped sweat from his brow and sighed deeply. He didn't really care that no one had been around to applaud him, but he hated the reason why. The whole campus was a ghost town. Everyone was at Nick Fox's funeral.

"Everyone except yours truly." Todd jogged over to the bleachers and wiped his face with a towel. He picked up a bottle of water and took a long swig. He knew he should have gone to the service, and not only because he wanted to pay his last respects to Nick. He should have been there for the twins. Elizabeth and Jessica had been there for him at Gin-Yung Suh's funeral; why couldn't he return the favor?

Todd closed his eyes briefly. Gin-Yung's face

floated in front of him. Not the vibrant, beautiful face of the girl he had fallen in love with, but the thin, wasted face of the stranger she had become. The brain tumor that had eventually claimed Gin-Yung's life had eaten away at her every day, draining her of life and laughter. In his mind's eye, Todd could still see how tiny Gin-Yung had become, dwarfed among the mountains of pillows in her hospital bed. She lay there, immobile, swathed in his basketball jersey. It had hung in folds around her emaciated frame. He shook his head to clear away the image.

Todd knew it was for the best that Gin-Yung had died. Her suffering had been so great that in a way, it had been a relief when the end had finally come. But he couldn't help remembering the happier days. He couldn't help wishing that Gin-Yung were still alive and happy and standing next to him right now, offering pointers on his game.

"I can't keep torturing myself this way." Todd groaned. Gin-Yung was gone; she had been for months. He had to get on with his life. Still, he wasn't ready to see another person he cared about be buried before his time. As much as he wanted to be there for Jessica, he knew he wouldn't have provided her much comfort. He would have been too busy reopening old wounds. Just like he was right now.

Todd picked up the basketball and spun it on

his finger. "This one's for you, Gin," he said quietly as he raised the ball above his head and sent it sailing through the air. It went wide and landed on the court with a dull thud.

"Great. Some tribute." Todd retrieved the ball and tossed it again, but his second throw was no better. He took a deep breath, focused all his energy, positioned himself on his toes, and tried once more, but it was futile.

"Forget it, pal. It just ain't happening today." Todd picked up his bag and tucked the basketball under his arm. His concentration was shot. The memory of Gin-Yung shadowed his every move, like an invisible opponent. Suddenly shooting hoops felt like a childish waste of time.

Todd glanced at his watch. It was time for lunch, and his stomach was starting to growl. He hadn't eaten anything since those slices of cold pizza the night before—maybe *that's* why his game was off.

But as he walked away from the court, he knew that skipping breakfast had nothing to do with it. Unlike a missed meal, his real problem wasn't going to be so easy to remedy.

Jessica looked down at the rose petals that remained in her hand. They had fallen from the bloom she'd tossed into Nick's grave, and now they lay, bloodred, against her delicate white palm.

With a convulsive shudder Jessica dropped the petals to the ground.

The pallbearers heaved their last shovels of dirt into Nick's grave. The priest closed his prayer book and whispered his final blessing. Nick Fox's funeral was over.

Jessica blinked and looked around her. She was alone. Everyone else had long since departed; even Nick's parents. She guessed they had all gathered in front of the church. Slowly she turned around and made her way toward the crowd milling about on the front lawn.

So many people, Jessica thought. Nick had touched a lot of lives in his twenty-four years.

The moment she reached the edge of the lawn, a throng of sympathetic friends surged around her. Their faces were a blur; their voices all mingled together in an unintelligible roar. Jessica felt assaulted by the attention. She looked around wildly for Elizabeth and the Foxes, hoping they would come to her rescue, but the crowd obscured her from view.

"Come with me," a voice whispered urgently in her ear. "You and I need to have a little talk."

Jessica turned to see Lila Fowler's familiar face at her elbow. She nodded gratefully and allowed herself to be led away.

Lila kept a firm grip on Jessica as she picked her way daintily back into the cemetery and through the tombstones. Jessica noticed absently that her friend was wearing a custom-tailored suit, woven of the finest cashmere, and handmade leather Italian shoes. But she wasn't impressed. Jessica shook her head, amazed that she had once cared about something so trivial as fashion.

"OK, this looks fine." Lila stopped in a small, secluded grove and turned to Jessica with a determined look on her face. "Listen, Jessica, I know what you're feeling right now." Lila's voice was as gentle as the breeze that stirred softly around them.

"You can't possibly understand what I'm going through," Jessica insisted. Her own voice sounded strange and thin.

Lila held up one hand to stem the flow of Jessica's words. "My husband was killed in Italy. Remember?" A small tear escaped Lila's eye.

"Oh . . . I'm sorry, Li," Jessica said quietly.

"It's OK. I'm wearing Lalique's new waterproof mascara." Lila wiped her lashes delicately.

Jessica looked down at the ground, ashamed. Of all of Jessica's friends, Lila was the only one who *could* relate to her situation. "I . . . I guess I just wasn't thinking."

"Forget it. Take it from me, you're not going to be thinking clearly for a long time. But Jessica . . . that doesn't mean you won't feel better eventually." Her large brown eyes were warm with sympathy.

Jessica shook her head. "I don't think so, Lila.

I never even knew what true love meant until I found Nick. We were even talking about getting married. . . ." She trailed off, remembering the pledge that she and Nick had made to each other during a secret rendezvous at a safe house in the hills. They'd promised each other that after the trial, they'd be together forever.

Until soon, Jess . . .

Jessica shivered as she recalled the raw emotion in Nick's voice. Would she always remember how he looked, how he sounded? Or would her memories fade with each passing day?

"Jessica, I felt exactly the same way." Lila reached out and gathered Jessica in her arms. "Everybody who's ever lost someone they loved feels the way you do now. I know that doesn't make it any easier, but believe me . . . you won't feel this way forever."

Jessica let Lila's words wash over her. She couldn't help but be touched by her friend's concern, and she was surprised and impressed by the depth of Lila's wisdom. "Do you really think that's true?" Jessica's blue-green eyes shimmered with tears as she looked at Lila with all the vulnerability and trust of a five-year-old. She almost hoped that Lila would suddenly wave a magic wand and make all her troubles disappear.

"Of course," Lila murmured soothingly. "Life goes on. You'll always carry Nick in your heart, but one day there'll be room for someone else too. Look at me and Bruce." Lila released her friend and held her at arm's length. "If someone had told me six months ago that I would someday stop mourning for Tisiano, I would have denied it. And if they'd told me that I'd be dizzy in love with Bruce Patman, well . . . I think I would have kicked them." Lila chuckled.

Jessica managed a small smile, but inside she felt conflicted. Sure, Lila had managed to get past Tisiano and fall in love again. But she wasn't Lila, and Tisiano wasn't Nick. No man in the world could compare to Nicholas Michael Fox.

"Speak of the devil." Lila looked over Jessica's shoulder. "Here comes Bruce. I think we need to get going. We've got an appointment with his personal shopper at Barney's, and he *hates* to be kept waiting." Lila swooped forward and pecked Jessica on the cheek before hurrying away, leaving nothing behind but a cloud of expensive French perfume.

Jessica turned to watch her friend join Bruce beside his shiny black Porsche. She kissed him—three times—and hopped in the car.

"How could I think that Lila understood?" Jessica muttered bitterly, wincing as the squeal of tires shattered the peace of the small graveyard. She was willing to bet that Count Tisiano di Mondicci was just as superficial and obnoxious as Bruce Patman. That was Lila's world in a nutshell.

The love Jessica had shared with Nick wasn't about money or status. No giant inheritance or trust fund could ever replace it.

Jessica looked around the secluded grove. The quiet surrounding her now seemed more eerie than peaceful. It was as if the life she'd once known had just vanished without a trace, leaving her empty and alone.

"I am empty. I am alone. Completely." Jessica's words hung in the still air for a moment before the sobs she'd held back all day finally punched their way out of her body.

Chapter
Two

_____

"Hey, buddy, slow down," Danny Wyatt called after Tom's departing back. "What are you doing, trying to set a new record for the five-hundred-yard dash?"

"Sorry . . . I just have to get out of here." Tom loosened his tie and slung his jacket over his shoulder. He walked briskly, anxious to put as much distance between himself and the funeral as possible.

"I understand," Danny said. "It's pretty tough sitting there and remembering that just last week Nick was alive and well."

"Yeah," Tom agreed absently. He squinted in the bright sun and fished in his shirt pocket for a pair of sunglasses. He was embarrassed to admit to Danny that as tragic as Nick's death was, that _wasn't_ why he was racing away from the church.

He just wanted to leave before Elizabeth embarrassed them both any further.

What had gotten into her? How could she push him away like that? Didn't Nick's death make her realize how precious life was? How important it was for them to forgive and forget and grab love with both hands?

"I'm starved. Want to get something to eat?" Danny asked affably. "We could grab some burritos at that new place."

"No, thanks," Tom replied shortly. He wasn't really listening to what Danny was saying. His mind was stirring with the memory of how it felt to touch Elizabeth again, coupled with the anger that had sparked from her eyes.

"Hey, what's going on? You look like you're getting ready to go one-on-one with Evander Holyfield." Danny gestured at Tom's furrowed brow and his fists, which were clenched by his sides. "If you were any more wound up, you'd explode. This isn't about Nick."

Tom relaxed slightly and looked at his roommate sheepishly. "You're right. I know I'm being selfish, but I just don't know how to handle this thing with Elizabeth. I honestly thought that I'd be able to talk to her today, you know, offer her a shoulder, but . . ." Tom trailed off, embarrassed by the fact that Elizabeth had called him on his intentions.

"Ah, that little two-step in the graveyard," Danny said knowingly. "I hate to say it, but Elizabeth didn't look too happy."

"She was furious," Tom admitted as he let Danny into his blue Saturn. Tom started it up, pulled out of the parking lot, and headed toward campus. "I really don't understand her. I was so sure that she'd realize how important it is for us to start over, you know? I mean, look at what happened with you and Isabella. . . ." Tom trailed off, hesitant to continue for fear of hurting his friend.

Danny's girlfriend, Isabella Ricci, had nearly wound up a vegetable after unknowingly smoking angel dust. The dealer who'd given it to her, Clay DiPalma, was now behind bars—at the cost of Nick's life. Thankfully Isabella was still alive, but she came out of it with amnesia. Tom knew Danny was having trouble coping; Isabella no longer remembered him or their time together. But he had also seen how Danny's love for and commitment to Isabella had grown stronger with each day.

"You're right," Danny said quietly. "Misfortune *can* bring people closer together. My feelings for Izzy are stronger than they ever were. But she doesn't even know who I am anymore." Danny swallowed painfully. "And I have to ask myself, is this *my* fault? Would this still have happened I hadn't been crowding her so much?"

"You can't blame yourself—"

"I'm not blaming myself; I'm just trying to give you some friendly advice." Danny looked out the passenger-side window. "I don't want to sound harsh, but I think you're making the same mistake with Elizabeth that I did with Izzy. You're suffocating her."

"Suffocating her? How?" Tom pounded the horn in annoyance. "As far as Liz is concerned, we're not even together anymore."

"But . . . you're still acting like, well . . . like she owes you something. And you're trying to force her to see things your way." Danny ran a hand over his close-cropped hair. "That kind of stuff doesn't work, Tom. You've gotta hang loose, give her some time and space. This Dana thing has obviously thrown her for a major loop."

"Understatement." Tom drummed his fingers on the steering wheel. "I don't get it. Why can't I make her see—"

"Hey. You can't 'make' Elizabeth do anything," Danny said. "Let her figure out things for herself. Don't back her into a corner like I did with Izzy."

Tom looked hastily away. The pain in Danny's eyes was hard to miss. It mirrored his own. Just a few short weeks ago life had seemed perfect. He and Elizabeth had been rapturously in love. Isabella still had her memory. Nick was still alive. What went wrong?

"Tom," Danny began hesitantly. "Could you

do me a favor and drop me off at the hospital?"

"Sure thing."

They drove in silence all the way to Sweet Valley Memorial. The moment Tom came to a stop outside the front entrance, Danny unhooked his seat belt. "Thanks, Tombo. Later."

"Later."

Danny stepped out of the car, paused, and leaned in through the window. "Hey, think about what I said, OK? You and Elizabeth have to let things work themselves out. Don't try to force anything, or you'll just drive her further away."

"OK." Tom nodded. "Thanks for the advice, Danno."

"Anytime."

Tom stared at Danny's departing figure for a few moments. He wished he could follow his roommate's advice. Tom wanted to believe things would just work themselves out. But as he recalled Elizabeth's parting words, he had to admit the situation was too dire to let slide. Tom had to do something drastic, or he'd lose Elizabeth forever . . . if he hadn't already.

Danny impatiently punched the door-close button. He had a book of Isabella's favorite love poems burning a hole in his jacket pocket, and he hoped that reading them aloud would help jog her memory. When the elevator doors opened onto the eighth floor, Danny bounded out into the Greenberg Pavilion—Isabella's new home away from home—and tried to ignore the butterflies that were dancing the mambo in his stomach. Would today be the day Isabella finally remembered him?

He sprinted the few yards to her room, 829-B. Danny stopped short at the open door. Isabella was alone, sitting in a wheelchair by the window. Her raven hair was loose, and she wore a Victorian-lace nightgown. The picture was so beautiful and tranquil, it took Danny's breath away. He couldn't even speak. All he could do was stare at her for a few minutes. Maybe if he just stood still and looked at her, he could convince himself that everything was normal. He could pretend that Isabella would turn from the window, her face would light up, and she would throw herself into his arms.

Isabella seemed to sense his presence. She turned around. A frown marred her lovely face. "Do I know you?" she asked tentatively.

His heart sank. "Izzy—it's me."

"Oh, of course!" Isabella's brow cleared, and she gave him a sunny smile. "You've visited me before, haven't you? What's your name again?"

"Danny." He struggled to keep his voice cheerful.

"Danny," she repeated. "It's so nice of you to keep coming around."

"Sure . . . no problem." He cleared his throat.

"Um, I thought that I would read to you a little today. Is that OK with you?"

Isabella nodded, wheeled her chair around, and gestured toward the bed. "Have a seat," she said cordially.

Danny sat down on the bed and took the book of poetry out of his jacket pocket.

"What a pretty book!" Isabella exclaimed. She reached for the slim, crimson-bound volume and turned it over in her hands.

Don't you recognize it? Danny wanted to cry. *Don't you remember we bought it together?*

He'd never forget the day he and Isabella had attended the Antiquarian Book Fair. They'd taken a long bicycle trip up the coast, which in itself was unusual. Isabella always laughingly proclaimed that she never did anything she couldn't do in heels, but Danny had thought she'd looked as gorgeous as ever in jeans and sneakers.

They'd stopped at the fair and wandered hand in hand before happening on the book of love poems. It was the first thing they'd ever bought together. After a picnic lunch on the beach, they'd read each other poems by the crashing surf until sunset. By the time they were finished, they were both so tired that Danny had to rent a car and load the bikes into the trunk. He and Isabella had laughed and kissed all the way back to Sweet Valley.

Danny blinked back tears. "It is a pretty book,

isn't it," he agreed quietly. He took it from Isabella and opened to one of Shakespeare's sonnets.

> *"Let me not to the marriage of true minds admit impediments. Love is not love which alters when it alteration finds, or bends with the remover. . . ."*

Isabella suddenly bolted upright in her chair.

"What is it?" Danny asked anxiously. Isabella was looking past his left shoulder. He turned and saw that Mr. and Mrs. Ricci had entered the room.

"Hello, Danny," Mr. Ricci said.

Danny stood up and put the book back in his jacket pocket. "Hi," he said with a smile. "How's it going?" His smile slipped a little when he realized the Riccis were carrying several large suitcases.

"Fine." Mrs. Ricci strode over to the closet and began removing Isabella's clothes.

"What's happening?" Danny asked, his voice rising in anxiety. Was Isabella being released? That didn't make any sense. She wasn't better yet. The doctor had said Isabella needed at least two more weeks of rest and observation before releasing her could even be considered.

"We've arranged to have Isabella discharged," Mrs. Ricci said as she folded a pink silk blouse and added it to the growing pile in the suitcase.

"We're taking her . . . someplace where she can

receive the best care possible," Mr. Ricci added, a note of caution in his voice.

"You can't!" Danny exclaimed. He looked at Isabella, but she sat placidly, unmoved, as if she didn't care one way or the other.

"Why not?" Mr. Ricci asked. He seemed surprised by Danny's outburst.

"Because Isabella needs familiar surroundings if she's going to regain her memory." Danny looked at the Riccis beseechingly. "She needs to see her friends. She needs to see her room at Theta house." *She needs to see me,* Danny added silently.

The Riccis exchanged glances. "I can see why this is a shock to you," Mrs. Ricci said, "but we're consulting a specialist in Switzerland. We feel Isabella would have a much better chance for recovery there."

"Can't you just give it a few more days?" Danny pleaded. "I know that if I can spend some time with Isabella . . . if she can go back to campus and sit in on some of her favorite lectures . . . any one of those things could jog her memory. Please?"

"Well." Mrs. Ricci looked at her husband. "There *is* something in what he says, John. Don't forget, I suggested it to you myself. Maybe we should let Isabella stay a little longer. It could prove helpful."

Mr. Ricci sat down on the bed and took one of his daughter's hands. "What do you say,

Isabella? Would you like to stay in Sweet Valley for a few more days?"

"Sure." Isabella shrugged. "It's warm and sunny here."

"OK." Mr. Ricci turned to face Danny and gave him a hard look. "We'll stay for now. I just hope you're right, Danny."

I hope so too, Danny thought.

Todd loaded up his tray with two thick sandwiches, a bowl of pasta salad, some fruit, and a brownie. That ought to keep him going for a while. He paid the stunned cashier and looked around for a place to sit. Not a hard decision. The cafeteria was mostly empty; he had his pick of tables. But he didn't relish the idea of eating alone.

"Let's see . . . who do I know . . . ?" Todd's eyes traveled around the room. His gaze swept over a group of guys who were busy with their laptops and some Alpha Pi sisters who appeared to be discussing hairstyles. He was about to give up when he noticed a beautiful, dark-haired girl sitting all by herself.

Dana! Todd's heart skipped a beat. Of *course* she would have skipped Nick's funeral. She was the only person on campus who had a better excuse than he did. Todd knew Dana a little; they'd had coffee together a few days ago, after her cello recital. But Dana's recital had been a disaster, and her dark mood had been painfully obvious the entire time. Still, even though the conversation had been stilted, Dana had managed to leave an impression on him.

Todd took a deep breath and walked over to Dana's table. He couldn't help but notice how put-together she looked. Her clothes were more subdued than usual; even though her fitted red sweater and long black skirt weren't particularly provocative, they still showed off her curves. Blushing slightly at the direction his thoughts had taken, Todd cleared his throat gruffly. "Mind if I join you?"

"Todd!" Dana flashed a smile. "Sure. Why not?" She moved her purse to make more room, and Todd immediately began unloading the contents of his tray. "Um . . . excuse me?" she asked tentatively.

"What?" He paused with a banana in his hand. "Oh—sorry. I'm taking up all your space, right?"

Dana shook her head. "No, actually. I was wondering . . . do you always eat so much?"

"No." Todd laughed as he squirted extra mustard on one of his sandwiches. "I just thought it might help my game a little. I was off this morning, and carbo loading usually gets me back on track."

"Your game?" Dana looked confused for a moment. "Oh, that's right. Basketball. I'm sorry, I'm just really out of it right now. You're, like, a star player, right?"

"Well, I wouldn't go *that* far," Todd said modestly.

"So what happened this morning?" Dana asked as she took a delicate bite of her chicken salad. "You didn't score?"

Todd glanced at her to see if she was joking, but Dana's sweet face looked perfectly serious. "Uh, well . . . I was just shooting hoops by myself. You know."

"Oh." Dana shook her head, and her silken hair flew about her shoulders. "I'm not that big on sports."

"That's OK." Todd reached for a soda. "I'm not that big on music . . . not *yet* anyway," he added when Dana's eyes registered shock. "But I want to be."

"Well, maybe we can teach each other," Dana said, her tone light and casual. Her gaze was glued to the table, but Todd was sure he saw her glance up at him for a split second.

Todd pushed aside his tray. "Maybe we can."

REBECCA FONTAINE
1900–1973
BELOVED WIFE

Jessica moved the ivy away from the stone and traced the chiseled words with her fingers. She had no desire to join the rest of the mourners.

36

She'd spent the last half hour wandering through the graveyard, admiring the tombstones and reading the inscriptions. She thought of it as meeting Nick's new neighbors. Smiling sadly, she walked over to one particularly old-looking tombstone and sank down in front of it.

LAURENCE SANDERS
1922–1989
BELOVED HUSBAND

The words swirled before Jessica's eyes. "Beloved husband. Beloved wife. Beloved husband," she chanted. "Oh, Nick, if only we had been married. We could have run away together, away from all this. If only you were still alive . . ." Jessica's voice dropped to a whisper and her shoulders shook with sobs.

Suddenly Jessica whipped her head around. She thought she had heard a noise, but the cemetery was completely hushed and still. Not even a bird could be heard singing.

Jessica stood up and brushed some dead leaves from her skirt. A twig snapped behind her. She spun around, but she saw nothing and nobody.

She ran her hands up and down her arms for warmth. Come to think of it, the cemetery *was* getting awfully chilly. A cold wind blew through, rustling leaves through the trees and whipping

Jessica's hair into a tangle. Dark clouds moved across the sky, threatening rain. Spooky. She *was* alone in a cemetery, after all.

But then—the hairs on the back of Jessica's neck rose. She had the distinct feeling that someone was watching her. "I don't believe in ghosts," Jessica said loudly. "I don't . . . not really," she whispered.

It's not a ghost. The thought forced itself into Jessica's consciousness. What if it was a person? No way. Who would want to follow her around?

Nick's killer. Nick's killer is still out there. . . .

Jessica fought back hysteria. She looked wildly around the graveyard. She needed to get back to the church. He couldn't get her if she was surrounded by other people.

No. If she made a run for it, she'd be an easy mark. She'd just have to take cover.

Jessica ducked her head and ran behind the nearest headstone. Safe—for now. She breathed a sigh of relief and closed her eyes. If she could just make it to the next grave, and then the next one after that, she could stay hidden until she got back to the church. She could—

A hand touched Jessica's arm.

She screamed.

"C'mon, Todd, you didn't *actually* score the championship-winning basket at the buzzer, did

38

you?" Dana asked with a giggle. "That kind of thing only happens in the movies." She and Todd had been sitting in the cafeteria for over an hour now, and Dana couldn't believe what a good time she was having.

She took a sip of her iced tea and leaned back in her chair. Her eyes traveled over Todd's face appreciatively. His brown hair fell across his forehead in a particularly appealing fashion, and years of playing basketball had given him a great build.

"Yup." Todd smiled. Dimples bracketed his mouth. "That's when I realized that basketball would be my life. When I play, I know it's what I was meant to do."

"I know what you mean." Dana brushed a lock of hair from her face and looked deeply into Todd's eyes. "Well, OK, not about basketball, but about cello. I love to lose myself in the music and forget about the rest of the world." Dana was silent for a moment. "Of course I have to be playing well. . . ." She sighed and fiddled with her straw. "That hasn't happened in a while."

"Things still pretty rough?" Todd asked sympathetically.

"Oh no, things are fine." Dana averted her eyes. "Just great." She tried to pump some enthusiasm into her voice. "In fact, I'm learning this new killer piece. . . ." She trailed off. "Oh, why bother pretending? Things are horrible, and not just with music either. I can barely get through pieces that I used to be able to play in my sleep, I'm behind in all my classes, my social life doesn't even exist, and I feel like a total outcast."

Whoa! What are you doing, girl? Dana chided herself. She might as well have put a sign around her neck that read Psycho. Rule number one: Never dump personal traumas on a guy. That was the next best thing to showing him the exit sign.

"Me too," Todd said simply.

"Huh?"

"I said I feel like an outcast too. C'mon, Dana." Todd's voice was heavy with irony. "You mean to tell me that you haven't noticed?"

"Noticed . . . what?"

"That I didn't go to the funeral either?" His eyes bored into Dana's with surprising intensity.

"I guess I didn't think about it," Dana said slowly. "I was too busy . . ." *I was too busy noticing how sexy you are.* . . . "Um, I was, um, too busy focusing on your basketball stories to really think about anything else," Dana stammered, a rosy flush warming her cheeks.

"Well, think about it," Todd said. He moved his chair slightly closer; close enough for Dana to breathe in his fresh-from-the-shower scent. "We're practically the only people on campus who aren't at Nick's funeral. I've known the Wakefield twins my whole life. You better believe I feel pretty bad

40

about not showing up." Todd sighed raggedly and ran a hand through his hair. "I should have been there to support them."

Dana wondered what it would be like to run her *own* hands through Todd's hair. *Stop it!* She gave herself a mental shake. *You're through with men . . . at least for a while,* she amended, noticing the way Todd's T-shirt clung to his biceps. "I feel bad about not going too, but it was a pretty clear choice for me. After the whole Elizabeth-Tom fiasco, I probably would have been escorted out of the church at gunpoint." Dana's blush intensified, and she felt as if her cheeks were burning. "Well, at least we know *my* reason." She gave a brittle laugh. "What's yours?"

"Look, whatever happened between you and Tom is in the past." Todd cleared his throat gruffly. "You can't be the only guilty party. . . . It does take two to tango, after all."

Dana wanted to believe him, but she knew how bad her behavior had been. She'd played dirty pool . . . and lost. "You still haven't told me your reason," Dana said quietly.

"Gin-Yung," Todd said simply. "I just didn't think that I could face another funeral."

"Oh, Todd, of course." Impulsively Dana reached for his hand.

"And I wasn't so lily-white either, you know." Todd looked away, but he didn't let go of Dana's hand.

41

Chapter Three

"Jessica! Calm down! It's me!"

Jessica shook with fear as she turned and looked into the pretty face of her friend Denise Waters. "Oh, D-Denise," she babbled in relief. "I was so scared. . . ."

"Scared?" Denise's brow furrowed in confusion. She helped Jessica to her feet and brushed some dead leaves from her dress. "What were you scared of?" she asked kindly.

Jessica looked over Denise's shoulder to where a group of her sorority sisters was assembled. "I . . . I was just a little freaked out," she stammered.

"Well, no wonder." Denise reached up and tucked a loose strand of golden hair behind Jessica's ear. "This is no time for you to be alone." As she spoke, the crowd of Thetas pressed forward, all talking at once.

Jessica clung to Denise tightly as the medley of voices filled the air. She couldn't make out what anyone was saying, only that they all seemed to be looking at her with pity in their eyes.

"Jessica." Tina Chai grabbed her hand and pressed it forcefully. The silk of her gloves felt cold and slimy against Jessica's bare skin. "I can't begin to tell you how sorry I am."

Jessica nodded dumbly. She resisted the urge to wipe her hand against her skirt.

"We're all sorry," Kimberly Schuyler echoed. She kissed Jessica's cheek, leaving a crimson mark.

"Jess." Alison Quinn elbowed her cohorts aside and swooped down on Jessica. Her skinny figure was swathed in yards of dull black. She looked like a scarecrow. Jessica shivered as Alison leaned over to peck her on the cheek.

"On behalf of all the Thetas, I'd like to offer our condolences." Alison inclined her head like a duchess. Her tone was clipped, and her mouth was pinched as if the words were distasteful to her. "We share your loss." Alison wiped away the single tear that snaked down her hollow cheek.

Crocodile tears. Jessica gulped. She stepped back to disengage herself from Alison's embrace. She looked back and forth among the crowd, trying to gauge whose grief was heartfelt, but everyone was a blur. Their faces blended into one, and Jessica felt as if she were staring into a sea of black.

Her knees buckled—if Denise hadn't been there to support her, she would have fallen. She squeezed Denise's arm, grateful for at least one true friend.

"Of course you know that one of the best ways to deal with one's own troubles is to come to the aid of others," Alison said condescendingly. "It also is part of the Theta tradition to offer support to those in need." She sniffed. "In any case, we're going to visit our dear sister Isabella Ricci now. Perhaps you'd like to come?" She raised a brow.

"I don't think that would be a good idea," Elizabeth declared as she joined the group. She pushed her way through the crush of Thetas and took her place at Jessica's side. "Jess, are you all right?" Elizabeth whispered. "I've been looking for you everywhere. Let's go home, OK?" She placed her hand under Jessica's elbow and began to guide her through the crowd.

"Bye, Denise," Jessica said quietly as she allowed herself to be led away. She was glad that her sister had rescued her. But as she walked out of the cemetery, she couldn't help remembering that the funeral might be over, but her life without Nick was just beginning.

"Hang loose, buddy. That's all you have to do. Just hang loose." Tom repeated Danny's words like a mantra as he strode across campus. He knew that his friend's advice was sound, but that didn't make it any easier to follow.

Just how long was he supposed to hang loose? Tom's brow gathered in a frown. He didn't know how much more of this he could bear. He could always hit himself on the head and knock himself unconscious—that should make it easier to get through the next few days. But barring a coma, he didn't see what else could put him out of his misery.

His stomach rumbled. Chow time. He swung left by the double doors of Waggoner Hall and headed toward the student union. With a heavy sigh he peered in through the window. It looked empty enough for him. The last thing Tom wanted to do was make meaningless small talk with whatever casual acquaintance he was forced to sit next to. Most of the Formica tables were free; just a handful of computer nerds, a couple of sorority girls, and Dana and Todd smiling blissfully at each other—

"What the . . . ?" Tom blinked twice to make sure that he wasn't hallucinating. No way could he imagine something that freaky. What was *with* that woman? Why did she have such an unhealthy obsession with Elizabeth Wakefield's men?

"And how come *her* love life is so hunky-dory?" Tom muttered. His face darkened into a scowl as he watched her reach out to hold Todd's hand.

For his part, Todd appeared to be totally smitten

with Dana. He held on to her hand as tightly as if it were a lifeline, and Tom thought that he could see tears in his eyes. She was probably laying some sob story on him. Tom was sure she had her whole "Tom Watts is such a creep" tale of woe down pat by now.

He watched as Dana leaned across the table and grabbed some napkins. Her red sweater pulled tight against her curvaceous torso as she did so. Same old Dana—about as subtle as a ton of bricks.

Tom turned away from the window in disgust. So much for lunch in the student union, and so much for kicking back and relaxing. Everywhere he went, there was something to remind him of Elizabeth Wakefield—correction, the *absence* of Elizabeth Wakefield.

One thing was for sure. Tom wasn't about to sit around and be miserable while *Dana's* love life was going full steam ahead.

"Screw hanging loose," Tom said. He swung toward Dickenson Hall, his heart lifting with every step he took.

"Isabella!"
"Isabella, over here!"
"Hey, Danny, over here!"
Danny turned his head to see what the commotion was about as he carefully negotiated his way down the hospital ramp with Isabella in her

wheelchair. The Riccis walked by his side, pushing a cart laden with suitcases.

Who told the Thetas that Izzy was leaving today? Danny wondered as the entire sorority descended on them. Instantly the air was thick with perfume and the chatter of excited voices.

"Isabella! You look great!" Mandy Carmichael cried.

"Divinely pale," Lila echoed.

"We miss you." Alison's tone was glacial.

"Are you OK?" Alexandra Rollins asked.

Mr. Ricci pulled Danny aside discreetly. "Remember, Danny, we're taking Isabella to the Stanhope Towers, suite 640. Please give us a chance to get settled first. Maybe you can visit in a few days or so."

A few days? Danny swallowed his disappointment, but he nodded. "Of course, Mr. Ricci," he said respectfully. He didn't want to do anything to jeopardize Isabella's stay—it had been hard enough convincing the Riccis not to take her to their home.

Danny turned his attention back to Isabella. He'd hoped that she'd appreciate the Thetas' attention or that she would recognize some of her old friends. But Isabella seemed frightened and confused by the loud noise and ceaseless chatter. Danny rushed to her side and patted her hand. She grasped it tightly.

"Who are all these people, Danny?" she whispered anxiously. "What's going on? There's too much noise. I'm scared. Please—get me out of here."

"Of course, Izzy." Danny gave the Thetas a regretful smile and began to wheel Isabella to the waiting limousine.

"I thought you said that all Isabella needed was a few familiar faces and places to regain her memory," Mr. Ricci said.

"W-Well, obviously it's going to be more complicated than—"

"I'm only giving you a little time with my daughter before I take her away. Understand?"

Danny nodded again, but inside, his heart was sinking. It wasn't just going to be complicated. From the look of things, it was going to be impossible.

"How about some pasta with my special tomato-basil sauce?" Elizabeth chattered brightly as she and Jessica walked into the lobby of Dickenson Hall. Actually, Elizabeth was doing the walking. Jessica was allowing herself to be dragged along, zombielike. "Or maybe we should have something really sinful, like ice-cream sundaes. I think there's some fudge sauce in the fridge."

Elizabeth wasn't really hungry, but she knew that it was important to get Jessica to eat something. Her sister had disappeared after the funeral, and Elizabeth felt sure that she hadn't touched food in days. She glanced over at her with concern, noting how thin and pale Jessica's cheeks were and how her eyes were rimmed with purple.

"Why don't you change out of your suit? You must be hot in that crepe," Elizabeth suggested, opening the door to their room.

Jessica nodded mutely but didn't do anything other than collapse on her bed. She drew the purple satin comforter around her and didn't seem to notice the mound of beauty products that spilled onto the floor.

"Uh, how about some tea first?" Elizabeth cleared her throat.

Jessica didn't. answer her. She just stared blankly at the walls.

While Elizabeth bustled about the tiny kitchenette, her thoughts were elsewhere. She knew the important thing was to stay calm. Jessica was a survivor, after all. She was going to get through this. As long as Elizabeth was there for her, Jessica would pull through.

"Well, here we are," Elizabeth said cheerfully, presenting Jessica with a steaming mug of mint tea.

Jessica stared at the bright pottery mug for a few seconds before placing it on the floor.

"C'mon, Jess." Elizabeth sat beside her on the bed. "I know you must feel horrible right now. But, Jess, life *does* go on." Elizabeth looked at Jessica's face for a moment before getting up and going over to her dresser. She grabbed one of her sky blue washcloths and a cake of soap and moistened them under the sink. Returning to the bed, she began scrubbing the mascara stains from Jessica's cheeks.

"Well, while you're having your tea"—Elizabeth glanced at the untouched mug—"I'll make lunch." She stood up and began rifling through the refrigerator. "Hmmm . . . well, tomato-basil sauce is out. How does peanut butter and jelly sound?" Elizabeth made a wry face at the lack of gourmet offerings. "I haven't had time to shop in a while, but hey, it's not so bad. We can pretend like we're little kids again. OK?"

Jessica remained motionless.

Elizabeth quickly made two grape-jelly-and-peanut-butter sandwiches and poured two glasses of ice-cold milk. She put the food on a tray and sat on the floor beside Jessica's bed. "C'mon," Elizabeth pleaded. "Try and make an effort, OK?" She pressed a sandwich into Jessica's hand and was relieved to see her sister take a small bite.

"I was thinking," Elizabeth said between bites of her own sandwich, "maybe we should redecorate the room a little. Some new posters would be nice, and we could ask the housing committee if they'd spring for a paint job. It's getting kind of grimy in here." Her eyes traveled over the walls as she spoke, taking in the many pictures of

Nick that were plastered over Jessica's bed.

Elizabeth cleared her throat. "So . . . what do you think? Do you agree we could use a little sprucing up in here? How about green walls with purple trim? Hmmm?"

Jessica turned a pair of dull eyes on her sister. "Sounds fine," she said robotically.

Well . . . at least she's talking, Elizabeth thought with grim satisfaction.

"I was back and forth between Gin and Elizabeth," Todd continued. "Gin was overseas. . . . I guess that was while you were involved with Tom. Elizabeth and I started seeing each other again. I didn't tell Gin-Yung about it." Todd's face was pale, and his mouth was set in a grim line. "Then she got sick, and I didn't know what to do."

"Sounds like we could both win the Nobel Prize for bad relationships," Dana said, surprised by how comforting Todd's hand felt.

"Heh—yeah."

Out of the corner of her eye Dana thought she saw a familiar figure hurry away from the student union. She dropped Todd's hand as hastily as if it were on fire. She squinted, but the glare from the sun made it impossible to see out the window clearly.

"What's wrong?" Todd asked. "Do you have to go?"

"N-No," Dana replied as she watched the guy round the bend near the science building. Well, whether he *had* been Tom Watts or not, Dana couldn't deny it was an omen. How could she even *think* about going out with a nice guy like Todd Wilkins? When it came to love, Dana Upshaw was poison. Damaged goods. Used and abused.

"Were you about to say something?" Todd smiled gently.

"No, nothing." Dana's heart felt heavy, and her voice was cold. "Nothing at all."

Jessica pulled her covers over her head. She was dimly aware that Elizabeth was babbling about some decorating scheme. Who cared? Who cared about anything? Nick was dead. That was all that mattered.

"I think we should think about a new rug too. A southwestern style might be nice."

Southwestern? Nick used to have a beautiful southwestern rug. Jessica could remember several steamy kissing sessions that had ended on that rug.

Oh, Nick, I can never kiss you again. . . .

The sandwich turned to sawdust in Jessica's stomach. She nearly gagged.

"Do you think we should get wall-to-wall instead?" Elizabeth asked as she noisily scooped up plates.

Jessica sighed. She wished Elizabeth would just

bury herself in her books or go to the library or something. Her incessant chatter was irritating. She wanted to be alone with Nick . . . with her thoughts and her memories.

"You know . . . I don't care about the rug," Jessica suddenly announced. *I don't care about anything at all.* She threw off the covers, jumped to her feet, and hastily peeled off her black dress. Jessica stepped on it with her muddy high heels on the way to the closet.

"Jessica!" Elizabeth gasped. "That'll cost a mint to clean."

Jessica's shrug was apathetic. She didn't care if the suit was made of solid gold. As far as she was concerned, the suit would only be a reminder of Nick's funeral. She didn't care if it burned. In fact, she didn't care if everything in her closet burned. "Could I borrow something of yours, Liz?" Jessica asked dully.

"Something of *mine?*"

Jessica walked over to Elizabeth's dresser and yanked open the top drawer. She smiled slightly at the neatly folded piles of polo shirts.

"This is perfect. Do you mind?" Jessica held up a pair of old khaki sweatpants with a torn waistband and a baggy gray sweatshirt that Elizabeth saved for scrubbing floors.

Jessica climbed into the sweatpants and went to look in the mirror. *Is that really me?* she thought with a catch in her throat. Her face was puffy from crying. Her normally brilliant aqua eyes had lost their sparkle. Her hair was dull and lifeless. It was hard to believe that just a few short weeks before, she'd been the image of the perfect California golden girl.

I don't care, though, Jessica thought disconsolately. *What does it matter if I'm beautiful if Nick isn't here to see it?*

Suddenly someone hammered at the door.

Jessica spun around with a shriek. "What was that?"

"It's just the door, Jess." Elizabeth went to open it.

"Don't!" Jessica lunged forward and grabbed her sister's wrist. "They're coming to get me. Don't open the door!"

"Jessica, what on earth are you talking about?" Elizabeth asked worriedly.

"Don't you get it? It's the killers! They're after me too!" Jessica dragged Elizabeth over to the closet. "Quick—let's hide!"

"Jessica, calm down, OK?" Elizabeth disengaged herself gently and headed for the door.

Chapter Four

Elizabeth paused for a second before opening the door. What if Jessica's paranoid fantasies were true? Nick *had* been assassinated by a hired thug.

Don't be ridiculous, Elizabeth chided herself. Still, she couldn't stop her hand from shaking as she flung open the door. When she saw Tom standing there, she realized she would have preferred facing a loaded gun.

"Don't slam the door on me, OK?"

"This isn't a good time, Tom." Understatement of the century. She uneasily glanced over her shoulder toward the closet, where Jessica was cowering.

"Elizabeth, please, just hear me out," Tom begged, looking at her with puppy-dog eyes. His shirtsleeves were rolled up, his paisley tie was loose, and his jacket was slung over his shoulder.

With his dark hair and smoldering expression, he looked like the Hollywood version of a hard-nosed reporter. She wanted to send him away, but she just . . . couldn't.

"We can't talk in here," she said. "We'll have to go somewhere else."

"Great." Tom broke into a grin. "Want to head over to the Red Lion?"

"No," Elizabeth said shortly. "This isn't a date, Tom. Just—just give me a second, OK?" She closed the door.

Jessica peeked her head out from inside the closet. "Is it safe?" she asked timidly.

"It's safe for you," Elizabeth said with a small laugh. "But I don't know about for me—"

"What do you mean?" Jessica withdrew back into the closet. "Are they taking you hostage?"

"Jess!" Elizabeth exclaimed. "Please, calm down. Everything's OK. No one's taking me hostage."

Maybe I shouldn't go out after all, she thought with a worried frown. Was Jessica really starting to lose it, or was this a normal reaction to grief? How was Jessica "supposed" to behave after Nick's murder anyway? Elizabeth had no idea. She didn't even know how she was supposed to behave with Tom half the time.

Elizabeth walked over to her sister and patted her arm. "I'm just going out for a few minutes with Tom."

"Is that all?" Jessica rolled her eyes. "So . . . OK, maybe you'll die of boredom."

"Exactly." Smiling in relief, Elizabeth picked up her brush and pulled it through her hair. *Jessica will be on track soon enough*, she thought. *She'll bounce back just like she always does. Maybe it'll take a little while longer, but in the end she'll be fine.*

"See you in a few," Elizabeth called over her shoulder as she closed the door behind her.

Tom practically sprang into action. "Where do you wanna go?"

"I don't have much time," she said sternly. "I don't really want to leave Jess alone. Why don't we go sit in the stairwell?"

"OK. How's Jessica doing?" Tom asked with concern as they walked to the stairwell.

"About as well as can be expected," Elizabeth replied. She tucked her skirt under her and sat down on the hard, cinder-block stairs. Tom sat down next to her. He was so close that she could see a tiny spot on his cheek where he'd cut himself shaving. "So . . . what do you want to talk about?"

"Elizabeth." Tom turned to face her. "You must know what I want to talk about. I can't stand being apart from you."

I can't stand it either, Elizabeth wanted to say. She craved his touch like a drug. But every time she thought of kissing him, she pictured Dana writhing in his arms, and she felt sick.

"Please, just give me another chance," Tom begged. "I love you so much. . . . *We* love each other so much. Don't you think it's wrong to throw that away?"

"But Tom . . . jeez. I don't want to go into this again." She took a deep breath and closed her eyes. "Tom, when two people love each other, they make a commitment to each other. And that doesn't include sleeping with other people."

"And that doesn't include you holding this against me for the rest of my life," Tom remonstrated. "Listen. Don't you think that you're being a little bit . . . I don't know, a little bit strict about the definition of commitment? You and I *were* broken up at the time. Cut me some slack, OK?" He rubbed the back of his neck and sighed deeply.

"*Cut* you some *slack?*" Her eyes shot sparks. "Tom, you betrayed me! You *slept* with Dana! You did things with her that we've never done." Elizabeth choked down a sob. "You've been more intimate with her than you've been with the woman you love—*claim* to love."

"Yeah. And whose fault is *that?*"

Elizabeth was silent. She could barely process Tom's words in her mind. All she could see was red.

"Look, I shouldn't have said that." Tom

touched her arm, and she jerked it away. "That was out of line, but—"

"*You're* out of line, Tom," Elizabeth agreed in a cold voice as she stood up and flung open the stairwell door. "You're a liar, a cheat, and a dog. You are *scum*, Tom Watts. Everything *about* you is out of line."

Slam.

"A large pineapple pizza, please. Extra heavy on the pineapple," Danny called as he leaned across the counter at Julio's. He wasn't the least bit hungry, but now that Isabella had been out of the hospital for a couple of days, she was allowed to eat anything she wanted. Danny was betting that the succulent aroma of freshly baked pineapple pizza would help jolt her memory. At least he *hoped* it would.

Anxious, Danny walked out of Julio's fifteen minutes later, carefully balancing the large box in front of him. He swung left and made his way toward Sweet Valley's most exclusive hotel, the Stanhope Towers.

"We're over here," Mrs. Ricci called. The Riccis were sitting on white wicker lawn chairs that overlooked a small pond on the Stanhope's vast, manicured lawn.

Danny walked toward Isabella, his heart beating faster with every step he took. Her face looked so beautiful—her ivory pale skin had a healthy glow, and her raven hair glistened in the sun.

The picture seemed so perfect. The air was full with the heavenly scent of honeysuckle, and ducks swam lazily in the pond. In the center of everything: A beautiful young woman sat surrounded by her two loving parents and the best that money could buy. It seemed impossible to believe there could be anything wrong. But it was clear from Isabella's blank gaze that things were still wrong. Very wrong.

"What's that delicious smell?" Mr. Ricci asked jovially.

Danny could tell that Mr. and Mrs. Ricci were making an effort to be cheerful. He joined in wholeheartedly. "Only Izzy's favorite thing in the whole world—after me, of course." He smiled at Isabella, but she gravely turned her head away.

Waves of anxiety took over. Isabella's response was *not* what he had been hoping for. Still, he had plenty of time to sit and talk to her today. And the pizza might still work its magic.

"We haven't had any lunch yet," Mrs. Ricci said as she took her daughter's hand. "Isabella, would you like something to eat?"

Danny could see worry lines pleating Mrs. Ricci's brow. His heart went out to her. He couldn't imagine how painful it was to know that her own child didn't recognize her.

"I'm not really hungry." Isabella sounded unenthusiastic. She pulled a plaid chenille throw more closely around her and looked at Danny suspiciously. "You came and visited me in the hospital, didn't you?"

Danny swallowed hard. "Every day," he managed to reply. "Every day, Isabella." He was silent for a moment, unsure of what to do next.

"Well." Mr. Ricci rubbed his hands together with false heartiness. "Let's see this famous pizza!"

Danny opened the box, and the delicious aroma floated out. Isabella sneezed. "What's that?"

"It's pineapple pizza, Izzy," Danny said softly. "Your favorite."

"It looks gross." She wrinkled her nose. "And the smell! Eew!"

"Don't worry, darling." Mr. Ricci grabbed the box and thrust it at a passing gardener. "You don't have to eat any."

Danny dropped his head and blinked back tears. He tried to reassure himself that everything would work out. But his heart nearly stopped when he heard Mr. Ricci tell Isabella that there was no such thing as that awful pineapple pizza in Switzerland.

"OK, everybody." Tom clapped for attention and winced as he took a swig of cold coffee. "Who made this swill?" he demanded. "Never mind. I've got more important things to do than draw and quarter the intern who botched the coffee." He flipped open his notebook and looked around the table in the WSVU conference room. "OK, people, I want to hear ideas. Phil?" He pointed at an intern with his pen. "Let's go."

Phil stood up and took off his glasses. He opened a folder and began earnestly explaining his concept for a series of reports on the student-assistance center.

Tom completely tuned out. Normally he loved the weekly brainstorming sessions at WSVU—they were a great way to get the creative juices flowing. But today Tom could hardly concentrate on half of what was being said. His mind kept replaying the scene with Elizabeth on the stairs.

". . . For one thing, the student center offers therapy. It used to be that the hot line was the only counseling service on campus. . . ."

Maybe I should go into therapy. I certainly need some help with my love life. Tom doodled Elizabeth's name on his pad, then crossed it out with a savage stroke. *Maybe she should go to therapy instead. She's the one with the problem, not me! Yeah! Next time I see her, I'll say, "You know what I think? I think you need some serious professional help, that's what I think!"*

Little by little, Tom became aware that the entire room was silent, waiting for his response to

Phil's story idea. His face flamed in embarrassment as he realized that he hadn't heard the last five minutes of Phil's presentation.

"Uh." Tom cleared his throat. "Sounds good, Phil, but I'm not sure it's enough for an entire report. It seems a little sketchy." Tom was pleased with his quick save, but he felt ashamed when Phil's face fell. Maybe he had just shot down some brilliant story idea. Totally unprofessional, and totally unfair to Phil. Tom made a mental note to make it up to Phil later. "Um . . . OK, next. Kat?" He glanced at a pretty, auburn-haired intern.

"I do have an idea, Tom," she said in her soft, hesitant voice. "But I'm not sure if it's good enough."

"Let's hear it before you pass judgment on it," Tom said. He leaned back and crossed his hands behind his head.

"Well, I was thinking about a feature on powerful women in the media. Think about it." Kat's voice grew in confidence as she warmed to her theme. "Twenty years ago there weren't any women covering the White House. Now it's commonplace."

"We could also profile some of the high-powered journalists who work locally," Phil chimed in. "Or even some of the ones who have a following on campus. I think it sounds great."

The group murmured enthusiastically as Kat continued outlining the idea.

Are they trying to drive me crazy? Tom asked himself. He knew he was being irrational, but that didn't stop the red-hot anger from building up in him like molten lava. They'd practically tailor-made a news story guaranteed to feature Elizabeth! Tom balled his hands into fists. *Elizabeth, Elizabeth, Elizabeth!* Even when he didn't want to think about her, people kept shoving her in his face.

"Tom?" Phil raised an eyebrow. "What do you think?"

"I don't like it," Tom snarled from between clenched teeth.

"Hey, Tom, no offense, but it's great," Michael Faraday, the chief editor, called from the other end of the table.

Tom gripped the edge of the table till his knuckles turned white. "I said, I don't *like* it."

"But Tom," Phil protested. "What's not to like . . . ?"

"I said no." Tom shoved back his chair and stood up. He towered over the entire table. "And I'm the boss around here—have you guys forgotten that? Remember, it's what *I* say that counts, *not* what some intern says."

Tom was ashamed of himself as soon as the words were out of his mouth. Everyone looked stunned, except for Kat, who looked as if she was about to cry. Tom felt as if he had destroyed months of hard work in a few seconds. It took a lot of courage for people to lay their ideas out on the table. What would happen the next time he held a brainstorming session? He'd be the only one talking.

Tom exhaled raggedly and ran a hand through his hair. "Look, guys, I know that 'sorry' doesn't cut it. . . ." He trailed off. "I—I'm out of here."

He grabbed his things and marched out of the room. He figured he'd head back to his dorm and get some sleep. Unless the ground opened up and swallowed him first.

"Hey, Blondie! Watch where you're going!" an irate driver yelled as he swerved left.

"Sorry," Jessica mumbled as she stumbled across the street. Who cared if she got run over? Who cared if she got herself killed? There was nothing left worth living for anyway.

Jessica staggered unsteadily from one block to the next. She'd come downtown to meet Denise and Lila for lunch. It had seemed like a good idea at the time, but now Jessica wasn't so sure. Her friends were nowhere to be seen, and she was alone without a familiar face to comfort her.

Frantically Jessica looked around her. The pretty streets of Sweet Valley were bursting with people. Moms pushed strollers, executives dashed back and forth on their way to important meetings, and couples strolled arm in arm. Cheerfully striped awnings fluttered in the gentle breeze, flowers in window boxes opened their faces to the sun in a riot of color, and the weather was warm and balmy.

Only Jessica seemed unaware of the beauty of the day. She shivered uncomfortably despite the mild temperature and wrapped the old, tattered sweater she wore more closely about her.

She scurried along the sidewalk, staying close to the storefronts and avoiding the other pedestrians. Jessica was sure that everyone was staring at her, so she let her long hair fall forward in an untidy tangle to hide her face from curious gazes.

"Where did Denise and Lila get to?" she muttered fretfully. She ducked into Lisette's, her favorite boutique, so that she could escape the crowd that surged relentlessly around her.

The bell on the door jangled as Jessica pushed it open and ducked inside. The scent of expensive French perfume wafted toward her, and she closed her eyes and inhaled deeply, glad to have found a safe haven at last.

"Ms. Wakefield!" the manager exclaimed. She welcomed Jessica with a beaming smile and an extended hand. "I'd been hoping that you and Ms. Fowler would stop by. We have some lovely things just in from Paris. Perhaps you'd like to look?"

Jessica nodded dumbly and walked over to the opposite wall, where a rainbow of silks and chiffon were displayed. Jessica plunged her hands in among the dresses and pulled a few out randomly.

Nick would have loved me in this, she thought disconsolately as she held a violet strapless dress up against herself.

"That would look perfect on you," the manager enthused, though her brow was knitted in a frown. "Ahem—Ms. Wakefield?"

Jessica stared at herself listlessly in the mirror before letting the dress slide to the floor. What did it matter if Nick would have liked her in it? He'd never see her again. Why bother being beautiful at all anymore?

"Ms. Wakefield, is something wrong?" The manager took a tentative step forward and held out her hand.

Jessica shrank back in terror, as if a snake were being offered her. *Why is she staring at me that way?* she thought with a shudder.

She broke out into a cold sweat. She ran to the door and flung it open, ignoring the protests of the manager. She dashed into the street and nearly collided with a young couple blissfully sharing an ice-cream cone.

"Excuse me," she babbled breathlessly. She looked at their love-struck expressions for a moment. A cry of pure anguish tore through her. Was it only a few weeks ago that she and Nick had walked down the streets of Sweet Valley sharing a double dip? Jessica stood rooted to the spot in horror, then turned and fled down the street.

She pushed her way past the sauntering throng of people, sure that everyone she passed was gaping at her. Exhausted and gasping for breath, she stopped outside the Italian trattoria where she was supposed to meet Lila and Denise.

Jessica pressed her face against the plate-glass window, searching for her friends. They were nowhere to be seen. Instead a sight met her eyes that made her cry out in shock.

Mr. and Mrs. Fox sat at one of the corner tables, looking sad but composed. She *had* to speak to them. They were the only ones who could truly understand her pain.

Jessica imagined them greeting her with open arms and taking her home with them to live. They would watch home movies of Nick and reminisce. And as the years went by and their devotion to each other grew, they would adopt Jessica as their surrogate daughter-in-law.

Blinking back tears, Jessica made a move to go to them. But as she did so, she caught sight of her reflection. Dark circles ringed her red-rimmed, swollen eyes. Her normally glossy, golden hair was dirty and wild. Her clothes—which she had pilfered from a pile that Elizabeth was planning to send to the Salvation Army—

were grubby and unkempt. She couldn't let Mr. and Mrs. Fox see her like this.

Jessica pressed her hand against the window. All her last remaining dreams vanished as she stood forlornly on the sidewalk, giant tears streaming down her face. She'd never be their daughter-in-law.

*Chapter
Five*

_____

Tom tossed a pair of sweats and a towel into his blue-and-white duffel bag and hefted it onto his shoulder. He closed the door to his room, left the dorm, and swung right by the fountain on his way to the gym.

After the disastrous meeting at WSVU, he'd gone back to the dorm to try and catch some sleep. But after staring mindlessly at the ceiling for a couple of hours, he decided that he might as well hit the weight room and see if he could work off some steam. It was either that or go crazy.

Tom flushed in embarrassment as he remembered the way Kat's face had crumpled earlier that day. He had to admit he'd been unprofessional and unfair to her. But why should he care about being fair when Elizabeth wasn't being fair to him? Just because he had slept with Dana—*ha!*

73

Dana was just as much to blame, if not more so, as he. Why didn't Elizabeth take her frustrations out on Dana instead?

Tom's mouth curled in a sneer as he saw the object of his wrath hurrying across the quad in his direction. He planted himself at the corner just beyond the library steps, where it would be impossible for her to avoid him. "Hey, Dana," he said with barely concealed hostility as she approached.

"T-Tom!" Her armful of sheet music went flying as she nearly ran into him headlong. Tom made no move to help Dana as she scrambled frantically on the ground to pick up her music from under the feet of passing students.

"Where are you going in such a hurry?" He raised a sardonic eyebrow. "Off to ruin some other guy's life?"

Dana paled beneath her makeup. "Tom, how—how are you? I . . . I haven't seen you around in a few days."

"You haven't?" Tom, feigning innocence, pretended to count on his fingers. "Oh, that's right!" He smacked his forehead with his hand. "You haven't seen me since you told Elizabeth all about what you and I used to do in bed together."

"You've got it all wrong." Dana's eyes widened in amazement. She clutched her music to her chest as if it were a shield. "That isn't what happened,

74

Tom. Honest. I—I just couldn't *believe* that you hadn't told—"

"This is a new look for you," Tom interrupted, gesturing at Dana's relatively demure outfit. "It actually leaves a little to the imagination. I never would have guessed that *Todd's* taste was so refined. He seemed to enjoy that tight sweater you were wearing when you were shoving your chest in his face in the student union the other day." He chuckled at Dana's stricken look. "Oh, don't worry, Dana. Your secret's safe with me. I won't tell anyone about this neurotic obsession you have with Elizabeth Wakefield's men."

"It's not like that. *I'm* not like that!" Dana protested, her face flaming. She looked as if she wanted to sink into the ground. "Todd and I are—"

"Let me guess," Tom interrupted savagely. "Just *friends?* Sure, and I'm the pope."

"What's happened to you?" Dana whispered. "This isn't like you, Tom."

"Let's not worry about what I am. Why don't we talk about what *you* are? You're what we like to call a *parasite,* Dana. You live off other women's men."

Dana flinched. She tried to step away, but Tom blocked her path. "Tom—stop it, *please.*"

"I bet you say that to all the guys." He lowered his voice. "But I *know* you don't mean it."

"Leave me alone!" she screamed.

Tom stared at Dana. Her eyes shimmered with unshed tears, and her face was drawn and unhappy. She trembled slightly, but she held her ground.

With a sharp intake of breath, Tom staggered back as he realized what he had just done. He had been impossibly cruel. His problems with Elizabeth weren't Dana's fault. The problems were his and his alone.

Tom swallowed hard. He knew he had to apologize. He looked up and became aware that he and Dana had made quite a spectacle. People were staring at them in openmouthed fascination.

"Dana, I . . ." He searched for the correct words. *Forget it—it's useless.* Tom reached out a placating hand. "Dana . . ."

But Dana just backed away from him.

"Dana," Tom said beseechingly. But it was too late. She turned and scurried through the crowd as fast as her bulky cello case would allow her.

"I'm *so* glad the physics seminar was canceled," Nina Harper exclaimed. She nibbled on an olive and flipped open the hand-lettered menu.

"Quick—a tape recorder! I never thought I'd hear you say those words." Bryan Nelson laughed as he spread butter on a thick slice of basil-and-sun-dried-tomato focaccia.

"I just mean that having lunch with you in town is a nice break from sweating it out over

76

Bernoulli equations." Nina snuggled up to Bryan in the red leather booth they shared at Sweet Valley's newest trattoria. How'd she get so lucky? Not only was Bryan the most brilliant guy she'd ever met, but he was also the handsomest. The warm flicker of the wall sconces threw his well-defined cheekbones into high relief and lent a burnished glow to his complexion.

"Besides," she began, tracing the rim of her hand-painted plate, "I need a little extra time today. I thought of an extra-credit project I want to do, and I need to discuss it with my adviser."

"What's it about?" Bryan looked intrigued. "Whatever it is, I'm sure it's really creative. That genetic-tissue-typing experiment you came up with in chem was one of the best things I've seen."

Nina sparkled with enthusiasm. "I wanted to do some work in optics. Really, it's not that impressive—I thought I'd just go a little further with something we'd already done in the lab." She plucked a flower from the vase on the table and threaded it through Bryan's buttonhole.

"I'm thinking of doing an extra-credit project myself," Bryan confided. "It's about—"

"Are you two ready to order?"

Bryan smiled up at the waitress. "Sure. I'll have the fried calamari to start and the linguine with clam sauce. Nina?"

"I'll have a mixed salad and the mushroom

ravioli." She handed the waitress her menu.

"So, anyway, I was saying that I have a little extra-credit project up my sleeve too." Bryan paused as if he were waiting for Nina to pepper him with questions. But Nina was preoccupied. She stared out the window with a worried frown on her face.

Is that Jessica Wakefield? she wondered as she looked at the disheveled figure who had pressed herself up against the front window. She looked so unkempt. Even worse, she looked . . . deranged.

"Try a piece of calamari," Bryan urged. He held a succulent morsel under her nose. "Go ahead—try it."

"Hmmm?" Nina suddenly came to. She hadn't even noticed that their appetizers had arrived. She accepted a piece of the calamari and turned back to the window.

Should I go to her? Nina wondered. She felt a brief twinge of guilt. She didn't *want* to leave the romantic restaurant to rescue Jessica. She *wanted* to sit with her handsome boyfriend and enjoy her lunch. Still, she could hardly believe she was seeing poor Jessica standing out on the street like Oliver Twist. Nina was about to push back her chair and go to her when Lila and Denise appeared and led her gently away.

Poor, poor Jessica, she thought sorrowfully. And poor Elizabeth too. Both their lives were falling apart, while hers was better than ever.

"Something the matter?" Bryan asked.

"No, actually. Nothing at all." With a bittersweet smile Nina dug into her salad. It tasted delicious.

A parasite.

Tom's words echoed in Dana's head as she slunk all the way to the music building. She unclipped the silver barrette she wore and let her silken hair tumble down to hide her face. The quad was teeming with students who had witnessed the entire Tom incident. Dana ducked her head down in shame as she moved among them, sure that everyone she passed branded her with the same iron that Tom did.

The worst thing about it was, Tom was right. She *knew* she was a parasite. She *did* have a strange thing for Elizabeth Wakefield's men.

Dana blushed hotly as the rest of Tom's tirade replayed itself in her mind. Had she *really* come on to Todd that hard in the student union? All she could remember was how cute Todd had looked as he grinned at her over his brownie.

No—she *had* been trying to keep it low-key. In fact, she hadn't flirted with Todd at all. In times past, she wouldn't have stopped at holding Todd's hand. She would have . . . well, she would have been all over him.

Dana shook her head and glanced down in satisfaction at the ensemble she had put together that morning. Ballet flats and an ankle-length skirt with a crocheted sweater had replaced her usual costume: Dr. Martens, fluorescent micro-mini, and skintight blouse. Still, she couldn't help feeling disconsolate. Even though Tom had been *wrong* about what went down the other day with Todd, he had been *right* about everything else. She was worse than a parasite—and more like a black widow.

She blinked back the hot tears that were prickling behind her eyes. She'd *always* poached other girls' boyfriends, as far back as she could remember. She wasn't a good student. She wasn't a good cook. She barely even knew how to make her own bed. The only things she'd ever been good at were flirting, plucking a few strings, and playing a little music. And now all that was falling apart too.

Elizabeth hurried across the quad. She'd been so concerned about Jessica that she'd barely been able to sit through her ethics in journalism class, and she was anxious to get back to Dickenson to see how her twin was doing after her lunch with Denise and Lila.

She knew that Jessica would be scarred for many months to come, possibly forever. But she also knew that her sister was a survivor. Elizabeth had seen her pull through tragedies that would have destroyed a weaker person. Spending time

with her Theta sisters had probably worked wonders for Jessica's recovery rate. Maybe she'd already put in a shopping hour or two.

Elizabeth bounded up the stairs, jogged down
the second-floor hallway, and flung open the
door to room 28. The sight that met her eyes was
a complete shock.

Jessica lay flat on her bed. She hadn't even both-
ered to turn down the covers. She stared unblinkingly up at the ceiling. She didn't seem any different
than she had on that first day after the funeral.

"Jess?" Elizabeth whispered tentatively. She
walked over to the bed and looked down at her sister. Fear gripped her stomach. Jessica looked dead.

Elizabeth sat down on the edge of the bed and
stroked her sister's hair. "Jess . . . how did the
lunch go?"

"Lunch?" Jessica repeated the word as if it were
foreign to her. "Oh, right. Lunch." She paused. "I
didn't have any lunch. Lila and Denise brought me
back here instead. I think I was crying too hard."
She blinked slowly. "I don't know why I wanted to
go into town in the first place. I don't think I ever
want to get out of bed again." She rolled over and
faced the wall, scattering a small mountain of wet
Kleenex as she did so.

Elizabeth looked at the pile of tissues in alarm.
"What do you mean, crying too hard?" she asked,
struggling to stay calm. She put a hand on Jessica's

slim shoulder and turned her sister back to face her.

Jessica shrugged and began chewing at her cuticles.

"Look at this." Elizabeth grabbed her hand in mock horror. "Is this Jessica Wakefield's hand? Jess, I haven't seen your nails look like this since we were kids. I'll tell you what." She stood up and walked over to her dresser, where she began rummaging through her pink-and-white makeup bag. "I'll give you a manicure, and you tell me what happened when you went to meet Lila and Denise."

As far as Elizabeth was concerned, few things were less important than the state of her sister's nails. But Jessica appeared almost totally catatonic. Maybe a little pampering would get her to open up.

"Hmmm." Elizabeth pondered the contents of her beauty bag. "Looks like I'll have to raid yours. I'm fresh out of nail polish." She made an effort to keep her voice bright and cheerful as she moved over to Jessica's dresser. Elizabeth grabbed the nearest bottle of polish and a file and went back to the bed.

"So." She took Jessica's hand in her own and began to shape her nails into smooth ovals. "Why don't you tell me about your trip downtown?"

"There's nothing to tell." Jessica turned her head to face Elizabeth. "I got there early. People were staring at me. I saw the Foxes. I'm never going to be their daughter-in-law. Isn't that sad?"

"Uh-huh." Elizabeth tried to decipher Jessica's ramblings as she shook the bottle of nail polish and began applying the pale pink color to Jessica's nails in smooth, even strokes. "Who was staring at you, exactly?" she asked.

"Everybody," Jessica said dully. "They're all watching me. Always."

"Did you get any work done?" Anthony Davidovic looked up expectantly from his perch on an old director's chair as Dana entered the studio.

Dana shrugged.

Anthony's gray eyes were stern behind his wire-rimmed glasses. Anthony was one of Dana's favorite teachers and usually very kind, but Dana knew that she was becoming a disappointment to him.

Great, someone else who won't be sending me a birthday card, she thought unhappily as she sat down on a metal chair and arranged her music on the stand.

"I'd like to put away the Beethoven for a while." Anthony gestured to the composition book that Dana was flipping through. "I think we should go back and practice the Bach suites."

Dana gulped, humiliated. Nodding mutely, she put the Beethoven book away and grabbed her volume of baroque composers. Her cheeks burned as she opened to the first suite. Although the Bach was beautiful, it was in no way as technically demanding as the Beethoven.

She opened her cello case and gently drew her instrument out from the quilted satin lining. She paused for a second, took a deep breath, and drew her bow across the strings. It sounded like a cat howling.

Dana winced in embarrassment but gamely kept going. She was acutely aware of the look of shock on Anthony's face, which did nothing for her confidence. Dana missed a chord and got confused in her fingering.

"Dana!" Anthony exclaimed as he held up a hand to stop the noise. "What's going on here? Have you even *touched* your cello since the last time we met? You used to play this kind of stuff—"

"In my sleep. I know, I know." Dana shook her head in chagrin. "Sorry. Practice hasn't been going well the last couple of days." *Try the last couple of weeks,* she amended silently.

"I really think that this lesson is a waste of time." Anthony shook his head sadly. "I've loved teaching you, Dana. You're one of the most talented and hardworking students I've ever met. But you've got to get a grip. You know you're going to have to work harder if you want to keep your scholarship." His voice was gentle but firm.

"I know." Dana hung her head. She couldn't

bear to look him in the eyes. She didn't know what she disliked more: Anthony's disapproval or Anthony's pity.

"I'm going to let you work by yourself for a while." Anthony stood up and reached for his tweed jacket. "We'll have a lesson again in a few days. Try to do some limbering exercises—your fingering is a little stiff. And don't forget to work on your scales. Remember, even Casals did two hours of scales a day."

He smiled kindly as he opened the door. "Look, Dana. I've seen you go through a lot of emotional ups and downs since I've been here. I'm sure that you'll pull through this. Just don't forget to practice. Otherwise there's no reason for me to keep tutoring you."

Dana groaned as the door shut behind him. "Great! What's next? An eviction notice?" she asked bitterly. Her bow dangled uselessly from her hands, and for a brief moment she considered running up to the roof and throwing her cello off it.

"My cello's not the problem," she muttered. "I am." She took a deep breath and found her center of concentration. Then Dana did some flexibility exercises, shaking her wrists to get the circulation going.

"C'mon, you've played these a million times before," she urged herself. "Just relax and you'll be fine." She drew her bow across the strings once more.

This time the horrible sounds that jolted the studio weren't her own. The sound was coming from one of the adjacent practice rooms. Although the walls in each room were padded, they weren't completely soundproof. Whoever was making the racket needed to be banned from even *touching* an instrument. It sounded as if a herd of wild elephants had been let loose in the other room and an oompah band was keeping it company.

Dana threw down her bow in frustration. No way could she practice with that ugly a distraction. She stomped furiously out of the studio, determined to stop the noise.

"What's going on in here?" she demanded as she threw open the door of the adjoining room, revealing Todd Wilkins's stunned face.

Chapter Six

"What's this about the Foxes?" Elizabeth asked shakily, desperate to change the subject. Jessica's paranoid outburst had almost caused her to drop the nail-polish bottle. She put it aside and began rubbing rose-scented lotion onto Jessica's chapped hands.

"I just thought that we could all mourn together," Jessica said sadly. Her face crumpled, and silent tears began to make their way down her already red cheeks.

"Oh, Jess." Elizabeth leaned forward and wiped a tear from her sister's cheek. It had about as much effect as trying to empty Niagara Falls with a thimble. The tears only rolled down faster.

What can I possibly do to help her? Elizabeth thought. She had to get to the library; she had an important research project due. But there was no way she was going to leave Jessica alone. Maybe if she could help Jessica feel useful, give her some busywork at the library or something, it would help her take her mind off . . . whatever.

"C'mon," she said briskly, twisting the cap on the polish and standing up. "We're going out."

"Out where?" Jessica seemed to shrink even further against the wall.

"To the library. I have a research project, and I want to keep . . . I need your help." Elizabeth helped her sister to her feet.

"My help?" Jessica slowly fumbled for her shoes. But she didn't protest.

Houston, we have a problem, Elizabeth thought with a bittersweet twinge. She'd never thought she'd see the day when Jessica Wakefield agreed to go to the library without a fuss.

Boy, talk about looking beautiful when you're angry! Todd thought. Drumsticks in the air, he watched Dana with admiration. Her hazel eyes were shooting fiery sparks.

"Was it something I said?" Todd asked timidly.

Dana kept glaring at him for a second. Then they both burst out laughing.

After her laughter subsided, she leaned against the door frame. "I'm sorry, Todd. I didn't mean to barge in here like that." Dana smiled apologetically. "I was having a hard time concentrating. Really, the smallest sound would have set me off."

She stepped inside the small rehearsal room and closed the door.

"Let's face it, I was making more than just a small sound." Todd scurried to his feet and removed some sheet music from a chair so that Dana could sit down.

"Thank you." Dana sat down and crossed her legs gracefully. "I didn't know you play drums," she said, eyebrows arched in surprise.

"I think 'play' is an awfully diplomatic way of putting it." Todd laughed. "I was just fooling around, trying to let off some steam. I figured that banging on the drums was as good a way as any."

Todd averted his eyes. He wasn't exactly lying to her. The therapist he'd been seeing at the SVU student-assistance center had suggested that he take up a hobby. And although Todd had given up on music, he did find crashing around on the drums a fun way to relax. But he couldn't exactly admit to a woman like Dana that he was doing this because of his *therapist*.

"So, how's practice?" Todd asked as he pulled a wooden stool close to Dana. He sat down and hooked his feet under the rungs.

"Let's just say that we're a matched pair."

Sounds good to me, Todd thought. He watched as Dana swung her legs casually back and forth. Even though the skirt she was wearing was long, it draped over her thighs in a particularly enticing way. He cleared his throat and forced himself to look at Dana's face instead, but her sparkling eyes and scarlet mouth affected him just as strongly.

"That bad, huh?" he finally managed to reply.

"Actually, it was considerably worse. You at least managed to sound like a herd of wild elephants, but I sounded like a cat being put through the spin cycle. Pretty pathetic, wouldn't you say? Especially when you consider that I've been playing for ten years." Dana fished in her pocket and drew out a silver barrette. With a sweep of her hands she piled her hair into an elegant French twist. A few tendrils hung down and framed her face.

Todd leaned back and crossed his arms. "I know what you're going through. Musicians, athletes—we all get blocked sometimes. I've had long stretches where I've been *totally* off my game." Todd kicked away the stool and began pacing restlessly back and forth. "You may not think basketball has a lot in common with music, but believe me, they're really similar. You have to bond with the ball or, in your case, with the bow. You have to totally give yourself over to the game or, I guess, the concerto or whatever. You can't hold back."

"That's it! Exactly!"

"But sometimes it doesn't work." Todd stopped pacing and knelt before Dana. His hands grasped the arms of her chair, and he stared at her with mesmerizing intensity. "Sometimes things don't come together in the right way. You miss a few shots, you fumble, you lose focus. *That's* when you have to recommit. You have to promise yourself that you'll ride out the tough periods. And believe me, Dana"—Todd's voice dropped an octave— "when you get through to the other side, you'll be stronger than ever before." Todd was silent for a few moments. Then he abruptly released Dana's chair and stood up.

"Wow," Dana breathed. "I had no idea we had so much in common."

Todd stopped in his tracks and thought over what he'd just said. He hadn't really thought about what he'd said to her—he'd been swept up in the moment, in the excitement of expressing himself. Dana was more than just a beautiful young woman who took his breath away. She was becoming a friend too. He couldn't remember the last time he'd had a conversation this meaningful with anybody. Sure, he and Elizabeth used to talk like this back in high school, and he and Gin-Yung—

Guilt slammed into Todd's consciousness with the force of a tidal wave. What was he doing having a great time with Dana when Gin-Yung was dead and buried? He tried to remind his conscience that Dana was just a friend. But he couldn't help thinking that he didn't have many "friends" who could do as much for a crocheted sweater as Dana did.

"Hey, an upright," Dana exclaimed. She jumped up from her seat. "I didn't even see this before!" She ran her hands over the glossy mahogany cover. "You want to give it a spin?"

"I think I've already performed enough for today," Todd said with a relaxed laugh.

"Nuh-uh." Dana plunked herself down on the piano bench and yanked Todd down beside her. "I won't let you leave here unless you play some Mozart with me."

"Mozart?" Todd drew back in horror. "Dana, I can't even play 'Twinkle, Twinkle, Little Star,' let alone Mozart! I'd mangle it!"

Dana trailed her fingers over the keys and gave Todd a mischievous smile. "Actually, 'Twinkle, Twinkle, Little Star' *was* written by Mozart." Dana began playing the familiar melody.

Todd threw back his head and laughed. He joined in, banging away on the keys with abandon. "Mozart didn't really write this, did he?"

"He sure did." Dana nodded.

"Well, there you have it," Todd said above the music. "Just what I was saying. Even genius has its off days. He probably wrote this one on his lunch hour."

"Speaking of lunch," Dana said casually, "would you like to grab a bite sometime?"

Todd stopped playing. "Sure. I'd really like that." But as his heart hammered with excitement, the same phrase kept hammering inside his head: *She's just a friend. She's just a friend.*

"I have to look through my notes and see what research materials I need." Elizabeth flashed a bright smile as she and Jessica rode up in the elevators to the eighth-floor stacks. "Do you think you could do me a favor, Jess?"

Jessica shrugged. She didn't much care what she did. As far as she was concerned, the only reason that she'd come to the library was because Elizabeth had dragged her. She could just as well be there as anywhere else. No matter what she did or where she went, it was all the same, and Jessica knew she'd just feel the same. She sighed and wrapped Elizabeth's blue cardigan more tightly around her.

"Well, here we are," Elizabeth said cheerfully as the doors opened and they stepped into the dim light of the stacks.

Jessica watched disinterestedly as her sister sat down on the floor and opened her backpack. She drew out a neatly typed sheet and put it in Jessica's hands. Jessica stared at it without enthusiasm. The words blurred on the page, and the call numbers made about as much sense as hieroglyphics.

"Do you think you could find those books

for me?" Elizabeth asked as she flipped through her notebook. "I'll be right here, Jess. If you need me, just call, OK? I won't be more than a foot away."

Suddenly they were plunged into total darkness. Jessica screamed and threw herself down on the floor. Nick's killer had followed her. Gunshots would ring out any second. "He's after us!" she cried.

"Jess, the lights in here are all on timers," Elizabeth explained. "Here. I'll take care of it."

In the darkness Jessica could sense her sister getting up and walking away. "Liz, no! Don't leave me!" she sobbed.

Suddenly the lights winked on. Elizabeth had walked over to a nearby wall and twisted a dial. "There's nothing to worry about, see?" She gestured around her. "The lights are set for fifteen minutes. The next time they go out, you'll know what to do."

Jessica scrambled to her feet. Her heart was still hammering against her ribs, and she couldn't shake the feeling that she was being watched. But the look in Elizabeth's eyes told her that everything was going to be OK . . . she hoped. Nodding silently, Jessica glanced at the paper without really seeing anything and began wandering through the stacks without really looking for anything.

Jessica had never spent much time in the stacks before. She didn't think she liked them very much. She glanced over her shoulder to make sure that Elizabeth was still sitting where she had left her, but even the sight of her sister hard at work did little to reassure her.

"Elizabeth?" Jessica's voice quavered. "I heard this place was haunted. Aren't there supposed to be ghosts up here or something?"

"Relax, Jess," Elizabeth called. "There aren't any ghosts, OK? Just find the books, and we'll go downstairs in a second."

But what if there are? Jessica thought, her eyes widening as she realized that the stacks could turn out to be the place where she and Nick would be reunited. She shivered in anticipation at the idea and looked around at the dusty old volumes with a new appreciation.

Nick, come back to me, she silently pleaded. *Show me that you still exist. Let me know that our love is stronger than time, stronger than death. . . .*

The lights went out again, but this time Jessica didn't scream, nor did she make a move to turn them on again. She could feel Nick's spirit right there beside her. He was coming back for her. She could sense his warm, sweet breath on her cheek. She could—

Jessica nearly fainted when she felt a hand touch her arm. It was as light as a butterfly's wing, as soft as cashmere. *Nick!*

"Hey," Elizabeth began gently. "What are you

doing, standing here in the dark? I showed you how to turn on the lights, remember?"

Jessica heard Elizabeth's footsteps, then the sharp click of the timer being switched on. The overhead lights sparked into life with a harsh fluorescent glare.

"Well, I've found everything I need," Elizabeth said. "Did you have any luck?"

Jessica shook her head mutely. Her stomach plummeted. She'd been so sure that Nick was there with her. But it was only her sister and no one else. Maybe if she tried a little harder—

"No?" Elizabeth smiled. "Well, that's OK. I think I can work with what I've got."

"But I didn't get you what you asked for," Jessica protested. "If we stay here a few more minutes, maybe—"

"It's all right, Jess. You tried your best, and that's what matters. C'mon, let's go downstairs."

Wordlessly Jessica followed her sister back into the elevator and down to the main reading room. Elizabeth found them two seats at one of the round, burled-walnut tables. She plunked her books down and pulled out a chair for Jessica.

"Hey, Jessica. How's it going?"

Jessica looked up, startled, as Matt Stevens, a guy from her history class, sauntered over to the table.

"I haven't seen you in class for a while," Matt continued. "You about done with that killer paper on the causes of the Russian Revolution? It took me about two weeks. I was stressing big time, but I finished it the other day." He patted his backpack. "Got it right here. It's a couple of pages under the required fifteen, but I think it hangs together well."

"Uh-huh," Jessica replied. She just turned and stared straight ahead. But Elizabeth seemed galvanized by his words.

"Uh, excuse me?" Elizabeth waved her hand. "Hi, I'm Jessica's sister, Elizabeth."

"Yeah, I can tell," Matt said with a laugh.

"Did you just say that Jessica has a fifteen-page paper due?" Elizabeth asked, her voice serious.

"Yup. Tomorrow afternoon. Well, see you in class." Matt walked off, clearly unaware that he had just thrown a time bomb in Jessica's lap.

As soon as he was out of earshot, Elizabeth leaned over the table. "All right—we have to mobilize here." Elizabeth sprang into action and dragged Jessica into the next room, where the computer terminals were. "We'll search the Internet. It's the fastest way." Elizabeth busied herself at the keyboard while Jessica stared off into space.

"Jessica?" Elizabeth sounded impatient. "You've got some major work ahead of you. Help me out here, OK?" She flipped through the various offerings on the web.

Oh no. Not that. Anything but that.

"Get rid of it," Jessica demanded as she stared in horror at the screen. She could feel the blood draining from her face. "Stop it. Turn it off!"

Elizabeth turned to face her, her eyes wide with surprise. "What's wrong, Jess? That's just the recent headlines from the *Sweet Valley Chronicle*. Their home page has a great search engine. They put the most up-to-date . . ." Elizabeth trailed off and turned to the screen. Right there was Nick Fox's obituary.

"I can't work, Elizabeth." Jessica shot her sister an agonized glance. "I'm sorry, I can't. I can't do it." She buried her face in her hands. "I don't care if it gets done or not. It doesn't matter. None of this matters at all."

Jessica slumped down in her chair and sobbed. Meanwhile Elizabeth kept on typing away.

Chapter Seven

"It's not fair," Elizabeth muttered as she stomped down the hall, her blond ponytail bouncing with each angry step. She'd never been late with an assignment for her art-history seminar before. Professor Young always seemed mellow enough. She'd have thought the old guy would have cut her some slack.

So far, Elizabeth's morning had *not* gone well. She'd been up all night frantically "helping" Jessica with her paper, only to fall asleep over her desk at six A.M. The fact that *Jessica* had been sleeping soundly the whole time didn't exactly endear her to Elizabeth, nor did the fact that she was *still* sleeping when Elizabeth had left the room at ten-thirty.

Elizabeth had dashed to Professor Young's seminar, arriving half an hour late and out of breath. But that hadn't been the worst of it. She'd been so busy writing Jessica's paper that she'd *completely* forgotten she had five slide explications due that day. Fortunately Professor Young had given her an extension, but not before he'd given her a serious dressing-down in front of the entire room. But nothing was worse than the feeling that no matter how hard she tried, she was powerless to help Jessica get herself back on her feet.

Elizabeth yanked open the door to their dorm room with a scowl on her face. There lay Jessica, blissfully asleep, snuggled under her purple satin comforter. At the moment she certainly didn't *look* as if she had any problems. Without thinking, Elizabeth slammed her backpack down on her desk in irritation. She winced at the loud bang it made. Thankfully, the noise affected Jessica about as much as would a feather that floated gently through the air before landing on a bed of marshmallows.

Elizabeth shook her head in amazement. She knew that Jessica was a heavy sleeper, but still . . .

She shrugged in resignation. She didn't want Jessica to wake up and be miserable, but she *did* want Jessica to wake up. Elizabeth knew that her sister was hurting, but she couldn't help feeling slightly irritated with her sluggishness. It was so unlike her. It was hard to stand by and watch.

With a sigh she turned away from Jessica, undid her ponytail, picked up her brush, and wandered over to the mirror.

Ugh. She looked awful. Elizabeth hadn't had time to wash her hair that morning, and it was stringy and lifeless. The purple shadows underneath her eyes clashed violently with her yellow polo shirt. She looked as if she hadn't slept in weeks. It took only one all-nighter with the Russian Revolution to do this to her. Imagine what the coming weeks with Jessica would bring.

Elizabeth turned away from the mirror in disgust and went back to her desk. She unloaded her books and found herself thumping each one on the desk with as much noise as she could. Why couldn't she stop herself from doing that? Thank goodness Jessica just turned over and snuggled in deeper under the covers.

She pulled out her desk chair and grabbed her assignment sheet for Young's seminar in one motion. But when she sat down, a giant yawn nearly split her face in two. *Ouch.* Her lips were so cracked and dry, they split in the corner of her mouth.

With a groan Elizabeth went out to the bathroom and splashed her face with water in an attempt to wake herself up. But beyond getting her bangs wet, it didn't have much effect.

She placed her hands on either side of the sink and stared herself down in the mirror. "Whatever

101

it takes, Liz," she told her reflection. "You and me. We'll get through this. Whatever it takes."

"Would you like me to read to you again?" Danny asked quietly. He scooted up to the edge of a blue velvet love seat and looked at Isabella. She was sitting up in bed, the fine, peach-colored linen sheets tucked carefully around her.

Isabella shook her head with a small smile. It was painfully clear to Danny that she still had no recollection of who he really was. He sank back into the love seat, and his heart sank along with him.

The hotel that the Riccis had selected was the last word in luxury. The minibar was stocked with every imaginable delicacy. The entertainment center was state-of-the-art, and huge bouquets of lush flowers filled the suite.

Danny knew that he should be happy Isabella's family was able to afford such beautiful surroundings for her, but he would have gladly traded the elegance of the suite for the humble surroundings of his dorm room. He would much rather have been sitting *with* her in his beanbag chair than sitting *across* from her in a prissy antique love seat. Most of all, he would have preferred to be alone with her than under the watchful eyes of Mr. and Mrs. Ricci, who sat perched on a brocade sofa next to Isabella's bed.

"Maybe something else, Danny?" Mrs. Ricci

asked sympathetically. She smoothed her daughter's raven hair back from her forehead. "I think Isabella's heard enough poetry for a while." She smiled kindly, as if she thought it would take the sting out of her words.

"How about we look at some snapshots?" Danny drew an envelope from his jacket pocket. It was crammed full with photos of him and Isabella and all their friends. Danny was sure that some of them, at least, would help to remind her of their life together.

Isabella's eyes lit up with interest as Danny spread the contents of the envelope out on the velvet duvet cover. "Who's this?" she asked, picking up a photo of Jessica and her that Danny had taken at a barbecue. Her brow furrowed in confusion.

"That's one of your closest friends," Danny said despairingly. "You two lived together for a while."

Isabella picked up another photo. "Is she a television reporter?" she asked, looking up at Danny for clarification.

Danny leaned over Isabella to study the photo. "That's her identical twin sister. She used to be a reporter at the campus station, WSVU. That's my roommate, Tom—they used to go out."

"Oh." Isabella let the photo slide through her fingers and lay back against the large, down pillows. "I'm tired. Do you mind if I rest?"

"Of course not." Danny fluffed the pillows around her.

Mr. Ricci cleared his throat. "Danny, can I talk to you for a moment?"

Danny followed Mr. Ricci over to the minibar. He felt as if it were the last mile. He knew what he was about to hear.

The aroma of freshly ground coffee was intoxicating. Jessica inhaled it deeply as she bit into her buttery croissant, which was oozing with honey. Mmmm . . . delicious. She couldn't decide what was better: the fabulous food or the fabulous boutiques. Whatever—Paris was her kind of city, and she was deliriously happy that Nick was there to share it with her.

"What do you think, Nick?" She leaned on the small, marble-topped table and looked deeply into Nick's gorgeous, jade green eyes. They were seated outdoors at a café by the Seine. "Should I wear the new black velvet, the green satin, or the pink beaded shift to dinner tonight?"

"Maybe we should just stay in and order room service," Nick suggested, his voice low and sensual as he reached for her hand.

"Sounds good to me." Jessica squeezed his hand in return. Her eight-carat diamond wedding ring caught the light and sent a shower of rainbow-colored sparkles dancing around them. "You know,

Nick, I was thinking. As much as I love staying in five-star hotels, don't you think it's time we got our own place? Some of those châteaus we saw in the Loire valley looked pretty happening—a little small, perhaps, but . . ."

Nick threw back his head and laughed. "Jess, just how much money do you think the witness protection program gave us? Those châteaus can be pretty pricey. But you do have a point." Nick faked a world-weary expression. "I'm getting tired of Paris."

"Tired of Paris?" Jessica shrieked. "Nick, are you crazy?"

"I was thinking we might zip over to Rome for a few weeks . . . or Vienna might be nice too. Sound good?"

"Sounds perfect," Jessica replied. She snuggled close to Nick and rested her head on his shoulder. The new French cologne he was wearing mingled with his own natural scent. Irresistible.

Jessica squealed as someone brushed against her. "What was that?"

"It was nothing, sweetheart. Just a waiter." Nick's voice was soothing, but his eyes were troubled. "You don't need to be so jumpy, Jessica. I keep telling you—we're safe now."

Jessica nodded, but her insides were still fluttering in fear. As blissful as it was being married to Nick and living in Paris, there were still nights when she woke up in a cold sweat. She had terrifying nightmares about being tracked down by hit men. Even the comfort of Nick's arms wasn't always enough to dispel her fears.

"Sorry." Jessica laughed shakily. "It's just so hard for me to believe that's all behind us." She reached for her coffee and took a fortifying swallow. "Wait—do you hear something?" She cocked her head and looked at Nick fearfully.

"No." Nick shook his head. "Look, why don't you—"

"Nick, can't you hear that?" Jessica interrupted him, her eyes wide with terror. "Someone's calling my name. They're on to us!" she shrieked. Jessica scanned the café wildly. She was sure that any moment now, she'd be staring down the barrel of a handgun.

"Jess, calm down," Nick said helplessly.

"No! Can't you hear them?" Jessica sobbed. She covered her ears in desperation. "They're after us. Oh, Nick! They're calling my name!"

Jessica felt a cold hand grip her arm, and she screamed.

"I'm going to be straight with you, Danny," Mr. Ricci said in hushed tones. "I don't think this is working. And I don't think it's going to work."

Danny swallowed painfully. He hated to admit it to himself, but Mr. Ricci was right. Isabella didn't seem to be any closer to remembering who she was than she had been the day she'd finally come to after her accident.

"I think it may be time to reconsider taking Isabella to Switzerland," Mr. Ricci continued as Mrs. Ricci came to his side. "She needs expert care. We can't deny her that."

"But Mr. and Mrs. Ricci—" Danny looked back and forth between them, his voice beseeching. "Please, just give me a little more time with her."

"You love Isabella so much," Mrs. Ricci said softly. "Don't you want what's best for her?"

"Of course I do!" Danny exclaimed.

"But with each day that passes, I can't help . . ." Mr. Ricci paused for a moment. "I can't help thinking that keeping her here is doing more harm than good. If we wait any longer, there . . . there may be no hope for her."

No hope. Danny stared into Mrs. Ricci's gray eyes. They were so much like Isabella's. He could tell that she was sympathetic to his plight, and he decided to put all his energy into persuading her.

"Mrs. Ricci, I don't think that we've really given this a fair shot. I mean—" Danny leaned forward, his voice growing in confidence. "Isabella's hardly going to regain her memory when she's in totally unfamiliar surroundings." He threw his arms wide, gesturing around the entire suite. "As gorgeous as this place is, it's completely strange to her. Just give me a chance to get her back to campus for a day or two. I know if Isabella has a chance to stay in her old room and see all her favorite hangouts, she'll snap out of this."

Mrs. Ricci looked at her husband. He appeared thoughtful, but unconvinced. Finally he shook his head. "I don't know, Danny. I think taking Isabella back to campus would prove to be too stressful for her."

"I agree," Mrs. Ricci echoed. She took one of Danny's hands between her own. "I need to be near Isabella. She has bad dreams sometimes, and I like to be close to her."

"I see." Danny nodded. How could he argue with that? There had to be something he could do. He stood and began pacing back and forth in frustration. As he did so he accidentally swept some of the pictures off the bed.

As Danny bent down to pick them up, a shot of Isabella standing on the porch of Theta house with all her sisters caught his eye. "Why don't you just let Isabella go to Theta house for the afternoon? I know her sisters wanted to arrange a tea for her when . . . when she was feeling better."

"It does sound like a reasonable compromise," Mrs. Ricci remarked thoughtfully.

"When do you think that this tea could be arranged?" Mr. Ricci asked. He looked at his daughter with concern. "I'm willing to take a chance. But I don't want to wait too long."

"I'm sure that we could have it within the next few days," Danny replied, his heart in his throat.

Mr. Ricci was silent for a few moments. Danny held his breath as he waited. At last Mr. Ricci said, "OK. We'll give you a few more days. Now, don't get us wrong. We're hoping this is going to work as much as you do. But I want you to know I'm calling my agent tonight to request three first-class tickets to Switzerland . . . just in case."

"Jessica! Jessica, will you get up already?"

"Huh?" Jessica sat up in bed and rubbed her eyes. Her dream dissolved before her, but not the fear. Her heart was still pounding madly, and now her arm was sore. Elizabeth must have been shaking her. "Why'd you have to squeeze so hard?" she complained.

"Because you wouldn't wake up otherwise," Elizabeth said.

Jessica stared at the walls in misery. If only Elizabeth hadn't woken her up, she'd be having room service in Paris right now with Nick. But Elizabeth had woken her up. Jessica wasn't sitting at a café in Paris; she was in her own bed. She didn't have a dozen glossy shopping bags filled with exclusive purchases at her feet; she only had her old pink nightgown. She didn't have Nick by her side. She was alone.

"Jessica, you should really get up and do something," Elizabeth said as if she didn't have a care in the world. "You can't just spend all day in bed, you know."

Jessica buried her face in her pillow, tears welling in her eyes.

Nina carefully placed the fine silver needle on top of the water in the beaker. When it floated calmly on the surface, she smiled. "I did it!" she exclaimed to Bryan, who was busy pipetting a solution into a bacteria culture. "I figured out the coefficient of surface tension!"

Bryan put his petri dish down on the stainless-steel lab counter and came over to join her. "You're a genius." He planted a kiss on her forehead and wrapped his arms around her.

"Mmm." Nina returned his embrace and tilted her head to look up into his handsome face. "In that case, do I get a special treat?"

"You sure do."

"Dinner at La Fenice?"

"Not exactly," Bryan said with a grin. "You can help me finish my experiment. I have to ask the professor something." He stepped away as Nina playfully swatted at him with the flat of her hand. "The protocol is in here." He tossed her his notebook and ran out of the lab.

Nina shook her head ruefully and flipped open the notebook. "Hmmm . . . this looks *pret*-ty challenging," she murmured, rolling up the sleeves of her white lab coat. She went over to the supply cabinet and withdrew a variety of test tubes, which she set up on the counter. She sat down on the bench and began mixing together several chemicals in a beaker, following the instructions in the notebook.

"Let's just hope I don't blow up the lab . . . eew!" She shuddered as foul-smelling fumes wafted off the solution she was stirring.

Nina set the beaker gently down on the counter and drew Bryan's notes toward her. His notes were famously thorough, and his lab reports were always immaculate. That was why she was so surprised to see some strange scribblings in the margin.

"What's this?" Her brow furrowed as she tried to decipher the squiggles of red ink. *Maria Lawrence*. One of the TAs, maybe? She racked her brains, trying to fit a face to the name, but she came up blank. "Whatever." Nina shrugged and turned the page, but there was even more doodling than before.

Nina felt a twinge of anxiety in her stomach. Just who was this Maria? And why was Bryan writing her name all over the place in red ink?

"Hey, genius, were you able to figure anything

out?" Bryan called as he came back into the lab, a set of anatomy charts under his arm. He looked so handsome in his lab coat, like one of the doctors on *ER* or something, Nina thought.

As she shifted over on the bench to make room for him, she found herself smiling at him. But she was still a little apprehensive about the mysterious Maria.

She gave him a sidelong glance. He appeared completely focused on the experiment. Then Bryan turned to look at her, as if he had just become aware of her not-so-subtle scrutiny.

"Anything wrong?" he asked, a quizzical expression on his face.

"Oh no. Nothing's wrong," Nina replied with a quick laugh. "Nothing at all." At least, she hoped not.

"C'mon, Jess," Elizabeth said as she stared at her sister's back. "It's time to get up." She forced her voice to sound cheery, but inside she was a mass of anxiety. Her semiconscious irritation with her sister had turned to guilt when she'd seen the terrified expression in Jessica's eyes. She reached over and drew back the purple comforter. "Jess? If you hurry, we have time for some croissants at the student union before I walk you to class."

Elizabeth reeled back in shock at the anguished howl that met her words.

"I'm *not* going to eat croissants! I don't *want* to have any croissants with you!" Jessica sat up and glared at her, wild-eyed, her hair a snarly mess. "I'm *never* going to eat croissants again!" *This is getting out of control,* Elizabeth thought in desperation. Jessica was only getting worse, not better. She pulled Jessica to her feet and placed her hands on her shoulders. "All right. Would you rather have a bowl of Special K? Would you like that? I'll fix it for you." She smiled weakly.

Jessica shrugged Elizabeth's hands off her shoulders. "I don't *want* anything," she said in a grim voice. "Correction—I *want* to be left alone."

"OK, Garbo," Elizabeth said, unable to stop the sarcastic remark from slipping through her lips. "But please do me a favor first, all right? Could you get dressed and get over to your history class so you can hand in your paper?"

"Paper?"

"Yes." Elizabeth propelled Jessica toward her overstuffed closet. "Not that." She yanked the tattered sweater that had been Jessica's uniform for the past few days out of her hand and replaced it with a striped oxford out of her own closet.

Elizabeth watched as Jessica climbed out of her polka-dot pajamas and into a pair of jeans. Listlessly she pulled a brush through her hair, but all it did was glance over the tangles. Well, at least she was *trying* to brush her hair. Obviously she hadn't for days. Elizabeth took that as a sign. Thank heaven for small miracles. *She'll pull out of this yet,* she told herself. The main agenda—for now anyway—was to get her going to her classes again.

Elizabeth packed the paper she had written, along with Jessica's books, into Jessica's bag. She helped loop the strap over Jessica's shoulder. "OK. Let's get out of here. We don't want you to be late." She grabbed her own backpack and a barrette and headed for the door.

"Where are you going?" Jessica asked sullenly.

"I'm going with you," Elizabeth replied hastily. She quickly twisted her hair up into the barrette and opened the door.

"What for?" Jessica dragged her feet as slowly as possible as they made their way down the long, orange-carpeted corridor to the elevators. Elizabeth figured helping Jessica down the stairs would take too long.

To make sure you actually get there, Elizabeth replied silently. She sighed as she led Jessica into the elevator and punched the button for the lobby. "Because I—"

"Don't you have your own life?" Jessica interrupted, a sour expression on her face. "Or are you going to be baby-sitting me all day?"

All week is more like it, Elizabeth thought as the doors opened. "I'm not baby-sitting you, Jess. I just want to—"

114

"Because if that's what your plan is," Jessica began, her voice growing louder and attracting the attention of several students in the lobby, "I don't want to be part of it! You're suffocating me, Elizabeth! Give me some space!" She accelerated suddenly, leaving a stunned Elizabeth in her wake.

Elizabeth stared at her sister in dismay as she raced through the glass doors and across the quad. Jessica had always turned to her in crisis situations before. What was going on now?

Maybe she's right, she mused, hurrying to catch up with her. Maybe Jessica did need some space. Who knew? Maybe this experience had matured her. Maybe Jessica was finally, really and truly growing up. But Elizabeth had to admit that Jessica hardly *looked* as if the tragedy had been a growing experience. She *looked* as if she needed TLC, and lots of it.

"Stop crowding me!" Jessica yelled as Elizabeth accidentally bumped her shoulder. "I told you, I'm fine!"

Why are you making it so hard for me to help you? Elizabeth wanted to ask. It seemed as though Jessica was trying to drive Elizabeth out of her mind. "I just want to be here for you, Jess. That's all," she insisted, forcing her voice to remain calm.

"Fine," Jessica snapped. "I appreciate it, but you're putting too much pressure on me!" She wheeled around to face her sister as they neared the entrance to the history building. "You don't have to walk me to my classes. You don't have to stand over me while I get dressed. You don't have to write my papers, and you *especially* don't have to wake me up when I'm dreaming. . . ." She trailed off uncertainly. "I've gotta go," she muttered. She ran up the stairs and into the building without looking back.

"Wow." Elizabeth exhaled heavily. "That was quite a speech! So you don't want me going out of my way to help you? Fine. I've got my own stuff to deal with!" She thrust out her chin defiantly. "I *do* have my own life, you know! Starting right now!"

Elizabeth spun on her heel and walked briskly back toward Dickenson. She wasn't sure what she was going to do next, but she knew one thing. Whatever it was, it *wasn't* going to be playing nursemaid.

Chapter Eight

"Twinkle, twinkle, dumdumdum, dadadada dumdumdum." Todd half-sang, half-hummed the tune as he strolled through the quad with his hands in his pockets.

It had been a long time since Todd had felt like humming, and he couldn't help thinking that Dana was a good influence on him. Todd recalled the look on her face when she'd burst into the music room and the way that they had laughed together afterward. He couldn't remember the last time he'd laughed that hard. Definitely not since Gin-Yung died.

Todd's happiness vanished, and he felt as if he had just been punched in the stomach. Was it fair to Gin-Yung to be thinking about Dana so much? He kicked a stone out of his path in frustration. He couldn't find an answer to that question.

What about Elizabeth? a voice in Todd's head reminded him. *What about what Dana did to her?*

Todd shook his head in dismay. He didn't really *know* what had happened between Dana and Elizabeth. Whatever it was, Tom Watts had been a big part of it too. And Todd knew how prickly Tom could get. There was nothing wrong with him liking Dana Upshaw. Was there?

"Hey, Todd, what's the good word?" Winston Egbert called out as Todd walked past Oakley Hall.

"Not much," Todd muttered. He slowed down and walked over to where Winston was sitting on the Oakley steps. Todd smiled as he noticed Winston's outfit: plaid Bermuda shorts and a Hawaiian shirt. Yeah, he could always count on Winston to cheer him up.

"What are you looking so down about?" Winston arched an eyebrow. "Didn't I see you walking around campus with Dana Upshaw the other day? You two seemed pretty cozy." He scooted over and made room for Todd on the steps.

Todd shrugged. "I wouldn't go that far. We're just friends." He ignored Winston's sarcastic laugh. "But I do like her a lot," he admitted. *Maybe too much*. He bent forward and plucked a blade of grass from the lawn.

"So what's the problem?" Winston asked. He watched as Todd cupped the blade of grass in his hands and whistled through it. "Hey, is that 'Twinkle, Twinkle, Little Star'?"

"Yeah." Todd threw the grass away.

"Pretty impressive. So, what's the problem?" Winston repeated. "You like her, and from the look on her face when I saw you guys together, she likes you. She's beautiful and talented, and *some* people might be misguided enough to think that you're pretty studly. Well"—he twitched his glasses on his nose—"not compared to *me*, of course."

"The problem is Gin-Yung," Todd said quietly. "The problem is Elizabeth. The problem is *me*."

"Ah." Winston crossed his arms in front of his chest and nodded sagely. "Now I understand. Ziss is vat ve call a guilt complexion, yes?"

Todd couldn't help laughing. "Yeah, Dr. Freud. You got it in one. I have a guilt complexion!"

"Why?" Winston blinked owlishly behind his horn-rimmed glasses.

"Because of what I just said, you idiot!" Todd sighed. "Gin-Yung, Elizabeth, et cetera, et cetera."

"Todd, I'm sorry, but Gin-Yung's gone," Winston said softly. "Is your being unhappy and single for the rest of your life supposed to bring her back?"

Todd was startled by Winston's insight, and he looked at his friend with respect. "Well, when you put it that way . . . I guess not. But what about the Elizabeth situation?"

"What about it?" Winston shrugged. "So Tom loves Elizabeth, Tom breaks up with Elizabeth, Dana wants Tom, Tom dates Dana. Oldest story in the book. What's next?"

"What about me?" Todd asked.

"What about you? You deserve to be happy, don't you?"

"I don't know," Todd said quietly. "I do know that I feel a little gun-shy right now."

"Look, Todd. Let me give some advice as a man of the world." Winston stretched his skinny legs out in front of him. "Denise and I just went through a hard time, but I really learned something from it. I learned that you have to hang on to love. If you feel something for Dana, grab on to it. Don't let go. From what I've seen of her, she looks pretty grabbable." Winston waggled his eyebrows à la Groucho Marx.

"You may have a point." Todd looked thoughtful. "But not about the grabbable part!" he quickly insisted, even though he knew that deep down, he *very* much felt otherwise.

"May? What do you mean 'may'?" Winston shrieked. "I'm incredibly sensitive and insightful. I should charge by the hour!"

"Huh?" Todd jumped up, startled. He'd almost forgotten. He *had* an appointment with someone who charged by the hour—his new therapist, Dr. Storey. "Hey, I've gotta hustle. But thanks for all your help, dude. Really."

"Don't mention it," Winston said as he leaned back to sun himself. "Just call me Doctor Love."

"So what do you think, Tom?" Phil looked at Tom expectantly. "Do you think graduate school is the way to go? Or do you think experience in the field is more important?"

"Graduate school is more important," Kat jumped in before Tom had a chance to answer. "You can't *get* experience in the field without going to graduate school first. Don't you agree, Tom?"

Tom smiled at the two interns as he chewed thoughtfully on his brownie. He'd been feeling bad about the way he'd treated both Phil and Kat the other day and had invited them out for coffee as a way of apologizing. They'd both accepted with alacrity, and Tom had sat with them for the past forty-five minutes as they discussed television journalism versus print, the ethics of revealing sources, and which Pulitzer Prizes had been undeserved.

There was just one problem. Tom wasn't able to concentrate any better today than he had in that disastrous meeting. Every time Kat or Phil would bring up an interesting idea, Tom would be able to listen for about ten seconds before his mind drifted off into Elizabethland.

"Well?" Kat nibbled on an oatmeal cookie as she waited for his answer.

"What?" Tom was startled out of his reverie. "Oh yeah, graduate school. Well, there are pros and cons. I think that graduate school has some good things to offer. . . ."

Yeah, Tom thought, *like maybe the women there are mature enough not to get all bent out of shape when their ex-boyfriend sleeps with someone else!*

"But probably the most important thing you get out of graduate school is another degree," Tom continued. He took a swallow of his cappuccino and considered the issue some more. "Really, though, in most cases, it's not much more than a piece of paper. For a lot of journalism majors, going to graduate school means you're really just marking time until you get a job. So if you can get a job in the real world without that piece of paper, I'd say you're better off."

There's one thing Elizabeth Wakefield is not capable of doing—living in the real world! Tom thought as he drew her face with the tines of his fork on the red-and-white tablecloth. *What woman in the real world could possibly care that her ex-boyfriend, who she was practically divorced from, hadn't talked to in ages, and whose phone calls she wouldn't accept, slept with someone else? Especially when she was back together with her high-school boyfriend on top of it all.*

122

"I feel the same way." Phil nodded as he dug into his pecan pie. "After I get out of here, I'm hitting the streets with my resume. What about you, Tom?"

"Huh?" Tom was baffled. He'd lost the thread of his own conversation. "I think that . . ." *I think that Elizabeth Wakefield is completely unfair, and I don't know why I still care about her so much.*

"I think that I'll probably apply to grad school *and* send out resumes," Tom fudged, signaling for the check. "I'll see what kind of responses I get. Look." He fished in his pocket for his wallet. "I've got to get going. What about you guys? Are you headed back to the station?"

"I have some dubbing to do." Kat stood up and grabbed her purse.

"Yeah. I better head over there myself and see if I can finish editing that piece on the asbestos problem in the gym." Phil stood up and stretched. "Thanks for taking us out, Tom. It was great." He smiled shyly.

"Yeah, thanks, Tom," Kat added.

"No problem." Tom smiled. He felt a little better about where he stood with Kat and Phil, but he wished that he'd been able to pay attention to the conversation for more than ten seconds at a stretch.

He walked out of the Red Lion with them and swung left as Kat and Phil returned to WSVU. His hands were deep in his pockets and his mind deep in thought. No matter what other problems he had in his life, Tom had always been able to bury himself in his work. But now he felt as if he had a terminal case of writer's block, and his behavior around WSVU lately could hardly be classified as professional. He kept mulling over his faults until a golden flash caught his eye.

Elizabeth. His heart thumped painfully against his ribs as he watched his former girlfriend dash across the quad toward the *Gazette* offices. Tom was struck by the determined look on her face. Now *she* certainly didn't look as if she was having trouble with her work. He felt sick with jealousy as he watched Elizabeth duck into the double doors of the building that housed the *Gazette* offices.

"That's it," he vowed. He was going to get back in the swing of things even if it killed him. He'd show her. He was going to scoop her so hard, she'd feel it for the rest of her life.

Tom turned around and hightailed it over to WSVU. He was on fire to produce a show that would make Elizabeth Wakefield sit up and take notice. The fact that he didn't have a clue as to what it would be about didn't bother him in the least.

Elizabeth adjusted her backpack as she headed up the stairs to the *Gazette* offices. Her earlier scene with Jessica still rankled, but Elizabeth was determined to get her own life back on track. She couldn't think of a better place to start than with the newspaper. Jessica was right. Snotty, but right.

The clacking of keys and shouting of instructions that greeted her as she pushed open the double doors to the newsroom was like music to her ears. The smell of the ink on the freshly printed daily edition was delicious. Better than Chanel No. 5, in her opinion.

She deftly wove her way through the maze of desks, avoiding interns who were rushing by with last-minute copy. She gleefully waved hello to the many colleagues who called out her name.

Elizabeth dropped her backpack and sat down at her desk. "Boy, it feels good to be here," she announced to the room at large as she leaned back in her chair.

Elizabeth grabbed a pen from the pink flowered cup on her desk and began going through the stack of mail that had piled up in her absence. She tossed aside the junk mail and made some notations on her calendar. "What's this?" she muttered, looking down in surprise at the fountain pen she was holding. "I thought I'd hidden this away." The pen had been a gift from Tom after they'd gotten back together. At the time Elizabeth had thought it was incredibly romantic, but now the sight of it only made her sad. With a shake of her head she flung it into the nether regions of her top drawer. *It's a good thing I didn't go back to*

WSVU, Elizabeth thought gratefully. How could she possibly focus on her career if she had to work with Tom Watts every day? The prospect made her shudder. It was time for her to concentrate on her writing, not lament the past indiscretions of no-good ex-boyfriends.

Elizabeth closed her eyes and imagined the speech she would give when she accepted her *first* Pulitzer Prize. She saw herself wiping away the tears as she described a life of single-minded devotion to her craft. Afterward the also-rans would be interviewed—Tom Watts among them. He explained how he'd missed the scoop of a lifetime because he'd been too busy "scoping for chicks" to follow up an important lead.

Elizabeth banged the desk so hard with her fist, the pencils rattled in their cup. Several coworkers turned to look at her. "I've had it with men!" she explained.

The women in the office cheered. The guys rolled their eyes and went back to work.

Elizabeth plucked a yellow legal pad from her drawer and with a look of fierce concentration began scribbling notes for story ideas. It didn't take more than a few minutes for Elizabeth to fill several sheets. She nodded in satisfaction as she perused what she'd written. Ed Greyson, the editor in chief, would *definitely* go for some of them. With a triumphant smile Elizabeth tossed her notes on her desk and leaned back with her hands linked behind her head to take a well-deserved breather.

Her gaze roamed around the newsroom. She sighed with pleasure as she watched her fellow reporters hard at it. *There's nothing more noble than being an investigative reporter,* Elizabeth thought soberly.

As she looked around at her colleagues, she wondered who among them would be risking their lives in years to come as they traversed the globe, reporting from combat zones and famine-ridden nations. Would Brad Turner be reporting from the trenches, or would he be covering the White House? Would Jane O'Donnell, the music writer, get her own show on MTV someday? She definitely deserved it. What about Jeremy Baker? She'd always admired his work.

Elizabeth craned her neck to see what Jeremy was working on. She could always count on him to be writing at least three stories at once. Elizabeth couldn't count the number of times that he'd scooped her, and she—

"What the—?" Elizabeth spluttered as she took in the spectacle that Jeremy was making of himself. Instead of frantically typing while issuing orders to some intern, Jeremy was drooling over a particularly busty blonde who was draped over his desk. If he were any closer to her, he could perform a tonsillectomy. But somehow she didn't think he was all that interested in her tonsils.

"Hey, Jeremy," Elizabeth called sarcastically. "Covering the scholarship-fraud story?"

"Hmmm?" Jeremy didn't look away from the blonde's chest. "Didn't you hear, Elizabeth? The cheerleading squad is going to be performing at the next Rose Parade. I'm covering it for the front page of tomorrow's edition."

"Men!" Elizabeth pushed back her chair violently. "They only think about one thing!" She scooped up her notes and headed toward Ed Greyson's office.

"Elizabeth!" Ed gestured for her to sit down in front of his desk. "I'm glad that you came in today." He took off his glasses and rubbed his eyes. Elizabeth could see how strained and tired he was. Ed was a consummate professional and a great leader, unlike *some* media managers she knew. He always burned the midnight oil chasing the hard stories. And, as far as she knew, he'd never chased after one of his female reporters.

"I'm glad to be here," Elizabeth replied.

"Good. 'Cause I've got a hot lead for you," he said, beaming.

"Fantastic!" Elizabeth smiled in return. "I've just been kicking around some great ideas myself."

Ed held up his hand. "Whoa! Knowing you, I'm sure they're terrific. But could you table them for a while? I'd like you to get started on this assignment."

"Whatever you say." Elizabeth felt a flurry of excitement. She wondered what he had in mind for her. An exclusive interview with the distinguished Nobel Prize–winning physics professor who was giving a series of lectures on campus? Maybe an exposé on how asbestos had been found in the gymnasium? Whatever it was, she knew it would be something she could really sink her teeth into.

"So, here it is." Ed paused dramatically. "I want you to interview as many undergrads as you can on this campus to find out what their secret feelings really are about . . ."

"Yes?" Elizabeth gripped the edge of Ed's desk. This was going to be good; she could practically taste it. "Their feelings about what?"

"Sex!" Ed announced happily.

Elizabeth's jaw dropped.

Jessica huddled in her seat at the back of the room. The paper that Elizabeth had written for her was safely tucked into her book bag, but Jessica couldn't bring herself to feel grateful for her sister's efforts. Not after she'd woken her up from that beautiful dream.

Maybe we'd already be on our way to Rome right now, Jessica thought. She closed her eyes and tried to see if she could fall asleep and dream of

Nick again. Unfortunately, even though the lecture was dull enough to knock out an insomniac, the hard wooden chair she sat in wasn't helping her along to peaceful slumber. Even worse, Jessica could tell that several of the students were whispering about her.

What are they looking at? She shot a filthy look at a couple of geeks who were sitting several rows in front of her. Twice now they had turned around and stared at her, pointing with their pens as they muttered comments surreptitiously. *Do they think I look strange?* She pleated the untucked hem of Elizabeth's oxford nervously. *Well, hey, granola guy, the last time I saw sandals worn with woolen socks was in an old documentary about Woodstock!*

Of course, if Jessica had been following the lecture a little more closely or been more aware of her surroundings, she would have realized that they were only following the professor's directions and looking at the large topographical maps that were plastered to the back wall, depicting the crop distribution at the time of the revolution. But Jessica *didn't* know that, and her skin crawled as she imagined the horrible things that the other students were saying about her. She shuddered in dismay and with a supreme effort turned her attention to the professor.

"By far the most important physical skirmish that took place during the revolution was when the Bolsheviks stormed the Winter Palace." Professor Turner gestured with his glasses for emphasis. "Close your eyes and imagine, if you can, the crowd, armed with only a few sabers against the soldiers with their rifles."

Jessica closed her eyes, but instead of seeing the Russian Revolution, she saw Nick. Instead of seeing soldiers fighting back the surging hordes, she saw Nick chasing after a thug. Instead of the uniforms of the imperial guard, she saw Nick in his leather jacket, looking unbearably sexy.

A sob escaped Jessica's throat. This time several students *did* turn and stare directly at her. She sat with her hands clasped over her heart and her head bowed as the images of Nick played on an endless loop in her mind.

"Nick . . . oh, Nick," Jessica whispered. Tears dripped down her face relentlessly, soaking Elizabeth's oxford. "Nick," Jessica gasped. Her voice was the only noise in the room. She opened her eyes. With a wild look around her, she sprang to her feet. Her eyes were blinded by tears, but she managed to grab her bag and throw the paper onto the professor's lectern before staggering out of the room.

"I just feel so confused." Todd groaned. He collapsed on the tapestry-covered divan in Dr. Storey's office and buried his head in his hands.

"Why don't you tell me about what's been going on since our last session, Todd." Dr. Storey looked at him kindly over the rims of her tortoiseshell glasses.

"I don't know whether I'm coming or going," Todd admitted frankly as he stretched his long legs out in front of him. "Last week I was sure that I was ready to take a rain check on life. Oh, don't worry," Todd quickly reassured his therapist. "I don't mean anything serious. It's just that nothing seemed to have any meaning anymore. We talked about that."

"We discussed the possibility of you taking up a hobby." Dr. Storey glanced at her notes. "We agreed it would be a good idea for you to pull back from basketball, take off the pressure. You said you might pursue some music lessons. What happened with that?" She looked up expectantly.

"Was that only last week?" Todd leaned back and rested his head against the couch and stared up at the green ceiling fan. "So much has happened since then." An image of Dana flashed through his mind. "Well, I bagged the idea of lessons, but music *has* made a big difference in my life the past week." Todd avoided Dr. Storey's eyes and focused instead on the many diplomas that crowded the walls.

"How so?" Dr. Storey raised her eyebrows.

132

"Did you buy some recordings? Listening to classical music can be very soothing."

"Not exactly." Todd ran his hands through his hair. He got up and paced restlessly for a moment before flinging himself into a large, plush armchair. "Is this OK?" He gestured toward the chair. "Or do I have to be on the couch?"

"Whatever you feel comfortable with. But Todd." Dr. Storey pointed at him with her fountain pen. "I feel like you're avoiding the real issues."

"You're right." Todd sighed raggedly. "The fact is, I met this really great girl. Well, I sort of knew her before, but I ran into her again at the music building." Todd paused for a second and drew a deep breath. "I just don't know what to do, Dr. Storey. I feel like it's too soon for me to be . . . feeling this way about someone. It's not fair to Gin-Yung's memory, is it?"

"What do you think?"

"Well, I think I really like Dana." Todd closed his eyes for a second and let the memory of Dana's perfume wash over him. "Maybe even more than like," he confessed. "But I don't think I'm ready. Besides, what if she doesn't like me? I'm not always clear on what vibe she's sending."

Dr. Storey held up her hand. "Let's take this one at a time, Todd. What's really bothering you?" She rested her chin on her hands and regarded Todd thoughtfully. "What's really the issue here?"

"Guilt. Fear. Loneliness." Todd threw up his hands. "The whole ball of wax."

"Where's the guilt coming from?"

Todd shrugged. "The guilt's from having the nerve to be interested in someone else so soon after Gin-Yung died. Plus Dana, the woman that I'm falling—the woman that I'm talking about," Todd amended hastily. "She wasn't that nice to my ex, Elizabeth, so I feel a little weird about that since *I* wasn't so nice to her either. The loneliness?" Todd spread his hands out in front of him in a gesture of futility. "That's self-explanatory."

"What's the fear about?" Dr. Storey probed gently as she jotted a few notes in her leather-bound book.

"I guess the fear is that Dana will reject me," Todd said quietly.

"Ah." Dr. Storey nodded and leaned back in her chair. "Most people are scared of rejection, Todd. I know that doesn't make it any easier, but what you're feeling is very common. I wouldn't be surprised if this young woman is afraid of being rejected by you."

Dana? Afraid of me? Todd shook his head in disbelief.

"It's time to wrap things up." Dr. Storey stood and brushed her skirt. "I think that you had a productive session today, Todd. It takes a lot to be able to open up in here the way you did."

"Thanks," Todd mumbled, embarrassed. He ducked his head and picked up his backpack, but his mind wasn't really focused on what Dr. Storey was saying. He found it so hard to believe that Dana would be as afraid as he was. But what did it matter anyway? He and Dana were just friends. And that was the way they were going to stay.

Chapter
Nine

Elizabeth took a sip from the cup of cappuccino that was growing cold by her elbow and nibbled on an almond biscotti as she reviewed her notes. It had been a couple of days since Ed Greyson had assigned her the story about campus attitudes toward sex, and until today she had only had time for a few sporadic interviews. Most of those had been fairly pleasant and uninformative. But today she had set aside several hours to work on the piece, and she had arranged to meet with some students in the Red Lion in order to get their views on sex. A few dozen people had stopped by, and while she couldn't say the results were particularly enlightening, at least she was gathering a lot of decent quotes.

Elizabeth blushed slightly as she read the list of questions she had prepared. Probing into other people's sex lives seemed awfully intrusive, but she knew that part of her job as a journalist was sometimes to stick her nose where it didn't belong.

"Hey, are you Elizabeth Wakefield?" a self-assured voice boomed down at her.

Startled, Elizabeth glanced up and into the face of a preppy-looking guy. He had an expensive navy blazer slung casually over his shoulder, and he had the kind of haughty demeanor that Elizabeth had come to know and love in Bruce Patman.

"I saw your flyer taped up over at the library," he said with a yawn. "The one asking for people's views on sex. I figured I had a lot to offer on the subject." He pulled out a chair and sat down, crossing one leg over the other with studied casualness.

My, oh, my. Elizabeth smirked. *He thinks he's all that and seventeen bags of chips . . . so to speak. This is going to be fun.* She flipped open her notebook and took out her pen, determined, in spite of her almost instant dislike of her subject, to give an impartial interview.

"What's your name?" Elizabeth asked pleasantly.

"I thought this was supposed to be anonymous." He signaled the waitress for a cup of coffee.

"I'd never disclose a source. But just so I know what to call you. . . . You don't *have* to tell me." Elizabeth watched as he made a production of adding sugar to his coffee and stirring it languidly.

"My name's Chip. Look, can we get on with

this? What do you want to know about sex?" He dropped his voice suggestively.

"OK." Elizabeth took a deep breath. "I guess the first thing I want to discuss is how much importance you place on sex in your relationships. College is a time when we all start to explore." Elizabeth ducked her eyes in embarrassment as she continued speaking. "And a lot of people choose to take their relationships on to the next level. Of course, not everyone makes that decision. . . ." Elizabeth paused and waited expectantly.

"What glacier did they unfreeze you from?" Chip asked, staring at her as if she had sprouted horns.

"Uh, excuse me?" Elizabeth spluttered.

"You're not one of those girls who hangs on to her *virginity*, are you?" Chip said the word *virginity* as if it were a rare disease.

"This interview isn't about me," Elizabeth said primly.

"I've got your number." Chip leaned back in his chair. His eyes swept over Elizabeth's neatly pressed button-down shirt. "You're like my last girlfriend."

"Oh, really?" The words fell from Elizabeth's mouth like chips of ice.

"Yeah. She was all hung up on her virginity like it was some special deal." He smirked at her over the rim of his coffee cup.

"So what happened?" Elizabeth asked innocently as her pen flew across her notebook.

"I wasn't going to hang with a girl who thought that holding her hand should be enough for a guy. I really felt for her, but we're not in kindergarten anymore. I dumped her and found someone who was willing to give me what I wanted."

"You dumped her?" Elizabeth repeated, unsure that she had heard him correctly.

"Yup," Chip answered with a knowing grin.

"And you just *found* someone else to sleep with?"

"Sure," Chip said breezily. "There are plenty of women on this campus who know what the score is."

"What's *wrong* with you guys?" Elizabeth slammed her notebook shut with such force that she upset her coffee cup. Cold liquid sloshed all over the table, but she didn't even bother to wipe it up. "Why is sex so all-powered important to men? Didn't the fact that you cared for your girl-friend mean *anything* to you?"

She noted with satisfaction that Chip was star-ing at her openmouthed, and she could see out of the corner of her eye that the rest of the room was watching her silently. But for once she didn't care that she was making a scene. "Why would you just toss away a relationship for *sex?*" she raged. "Sex, sex, sex! I'm *tired* of men only caring about *sex!*"

"Hey." Chip held up his hands in a placating gesture. "I didn't mean to get you all unhinged, OK? I'm sorry."

Elizabeth stood in silence. She refused to accept his apology.

"Uh . . . so do you want to keep interviewing me or what?"

"Oh, I think I have *quite* enough." Elizabeth flashed a sarcastic smile. "*More* than enough, thank you. Why don't *I* finish writing up my notes and *you* go out and 'find' someone else to have *sex* with!"

The entire coffee shop was silent. Chip stared at her for one long minute with his eyes bugging out of his head, then he shoved back his chair and booked out of the room as if Elizabeth were chasing him with a whip.

Elizabeth grabbed her materials and marched out, her mind already formulating the opening paragraph of her article. If she could give Chip only one thing, it was that he was honest. He had confirmed for her what she already knew about guys on the SVU campus. Now it was time everyone learned that there were other people with other points of view.

She ran across the quad, her blond hair streaming out behind her. She'd show Todd, and Tom, and every man on campus that it was time for them to get over their hormonal problems and realize that things like love and trust and companionship were more important than sex for sex's sake.

Elizabeth dashed up the stairs and flung open

the doors to the *Gazette* offices, on fire to get started. "And most of all," Elizabeth muttered with a fierce frown as she flicked on her computer, "it's time for people to realize that being a virgin doesn't make you a relic of the Ice Age."

Jessica wandered through the quad in a daze. She thought that she might go to the dining hall and grab some lunch, but she wasn't sure if she'd already *had* lunch or not.

"Or was that breakfast?" she murmured, a frown marring her brow. Whatever. It was hard keeping track of things without Elizabeth around to mother-hen her.

"Hey, Jessica!"

Jessica froze like a deer in the headlights. "Who's calling me?" she whimpered, looking around wildly, wondering if she should take cover by the fountain.

"Hey, Jess." Anoushka Koll caught up with her. "Are you going to the Theta tea?" She flashed Jessica a wide grin, and her eyes sparkled happily.

Jessica backed away uncertainly. She was sure that Anoushka was staring at her peculiarly, as if she were taken aback by Jessica's outfit.

What's wrong with my outfit? Jessica wondered defensively. She smoothed her torn cardigan down over the pair of wrinkled khakis that she had pilfered from Elizabeth's closet.

"Want to walk over with me?" Anoushka linked arms with Jessica and started to lead her over toward the lawn of Theta house.

"No!" Jessica blurted out. She withdrew her arm hastily, sure she could see pity lurking in Anoushka's eyes. "I don't want to go to Theta house with you! Leave me alone!" She backed away. "Leave me alone!" Jessica turned and ran.

Why was everyone bothering her? Why was everyone staring at her? Why couldn't they just let her be?

The back of Jessica's neck prickled with fear. She was sure that she could feel a pair of eyes boring into her. She spun around.

Jessica caught a glimpse of flashing green eyes and a pair of broad shoulders encased in a leather jacket before their owner turned the corner.

Nick! Tears of joy sprang to Jessica's eyes as she dashed after him in hot pursuit. Nick seemed to be making his way to Theta house; he was going across the lawn, at least. He must have gone to Dickenson. When he didn't find her there, he would have figured she went to Theta house! The thought that she would be in Nick's arms again in just a few minutes was enough to make Jessica nearly faint with happiness.

"Just a few seconds now," she babbled. "Just a few seconds and we'll be together again." Jessica flew across the lawn of Theta house in hot pursuit. "Nick! Wait! Here I am! *Nick!*"

Danny shifted uncomfortably. The grass was poking him through his pants, the endless chattering of the Thetas was seriously wearing on his nerves, and cucumber sandwiches were *not* his meal of choice. Still, he would have walked through fire if he thought it would do Isabella any good, and even though sitting next to Alison Quinn *did* rank pretty close to fire walking on his list, Danny was sure that the Theta tea would help jog Isabella's memory.

There's just one problem, Danny thought with a sinking heart as he watched Isabella drink a glass of lemonade. Isabella wasn't getting any better. If anything, she was getting worse.

Isabella seemed dazed and confused by all the noise and attention that surrounded her. She shrank back in her chair as her sorority sisters gathered around her, and she didn't seem to be able to follow the conversation at all. He'd thought Isabella would be so jazzed to see the Thetas again—or at the very least, she'd be moved by all the effort they'd made just for her. But she didn't seem to acknowledge that at all. Their efforts only seemed to intimidate her.

Danny looked around him. A large, pink, embroidered tablecloth had been spread on the grass

144

underneath a flowering apple tree. The cloth was laden with dozens of little tea sandwiches and several varieties of cookies. Lemonade and tea were being served, and Danny hadn't seen such fancy china since he'd last had lunch with his grandmother. He remembered how Isabella used to go hog-wild for all that frilly stuff. Why wasn't it bringing back memories? Why wasn't it even making her *happy*, at least?

"Hey, Isabella, remember, you used to be the official Theta house manicurist," Mandy Carmichael called. She thrust a bottle of nail polish at Isabella, who recoiled as if it were a grenade.

"Maybe we should hold off on the manicures for a while." Danny grabbed the bottle out of Mandy's hand. He knelt beside Isabella and stroked her hair. "Don't worry, Izzy," he murmured gently, but Izzy seemed to shy away from him also. Danny's stomach lurched terribly, and he fought hard to contain his disappointment.

"Hey, isn't that Jessica?" he heard Tina Chai whisper.

Danny followed her gaze and saw Jessica Wakefield stumbling across the quad. He hadn't seen her since the funeral, and he was shocked by the changes in her appearance. He watched in horrified fascination as Jessica turned left and lurched crookedly toward them. She seemed intent on following a guy in a leather jacket who looked vaguely like Nick. *Is she going to make it?* Danny wondered uneasily. Jessica's progress was anything but steady, and Danny saw that she was having a hard time keeping upright. Suddenly she teetered, and with her arms flailing wildly about her, fell.

Danny scrambled to his feet in an instant and sprinted across the lawn, where Jessica lay face-down on the grass.

"Jessica?" He bent down and helped her to her feet. "Are you all right?" He winced at the stupidity of his question, but Jessica didn't even appear to hear him.

"I have to follow him," she babbled. Her eyes looked unfocused.

"Jess?" Danny wrapped a steadying arm around her as she rocked back and forth on her heels. "Why don't you let me take you home?"

"I have to follow him!" Jessica cried. She pushed Danny away with a sudden burst of strength and resumed running across the lawn.

"Poor, poor Jess," Danny murmured as he made his way slowly back to where Isabella sat under the willow tree. "What's happening to everybody? First Isabella, now Jessica, not to mention Nick." He sighed unhappily.

"You're very kind." Isabella's musical voice was so quiet, Danny had hardly heard her.

"Excuse me?" He looked at her in surprise as he took his seat on the lawn by her side.

"I said you're very kind. Not everybody would help a girl that way." Her gray eyes shone with respect, and her smile was small but sweet. "You're a really nice man, Danny. I like you a lot."

Danny's heart leaped with joy. Maybe Isabella couldn't remember who he was, but she was starting to like him all the same. He took her hand and held it gently. When she didn't withdraw it, a small thrill went through him. When Isabella's smile grew, he smiled back. And when he took a bite of a watercress sandwich, he didn't even wince.

"Todd!" Dana exclaimed in surprise. "What are you doing in here? Coming to play the drums again? Or were you hoping to do a command performance of Mozart?"

Dana smiled warmly at Todd as they stood just inside the entrance to the music building. The entrance was a hive of activity, with students rushing back and forth carrying various instruments. A guy rushed by tangled in a giant tuba, and Dana stepped closer to Todd to avoid being sideswiped by a pair of kettledrums.

What's Todd doing here? Dana wondered as she was inadvertently pressed against him. *Did he come to see me?* Her heart fluttered at the prospect. She could feel *his* heart beating beneath the striped jersey he wore. She could also feel the swell of his biceps as he steadied her with his arms.

"Neither." Todd let go of Dana and gestured toward the bulletin board. "I was hoping to see if there were any good recitals coming up. Are you going to be playing again anytime soon?"

"No, not for a while," Dana replied, but the wheels were spinning inside her mind. Could he really have shown up just for that? Was she just flattering herself to think that he was actually hoping to see her?

"So, what are *you* doing here?" Todd raised an eyebrow. "Stupid question." He pointed at her cello case. "Are you just getting started or just finishing?"

"Just getting started," Dana replied. She paused, unsure of what to say next.

"Really?" Todd leaned back against the cork bulletin board. "Feel like having an audience?"

Do I? Dana asked herself. There was no denying that Todd looked extremely appealing at that moment, and she shivered slightly at the way his hands had felt on her shoulders. But she was also terrified of how she might sound. Her last practice with an audience had been in front of Anthony. What a disaster that had been! Dana inadvertently frowned at the memory.

"I take it that's a no?" Todd asked, a note of disappointment in his voice.

"What? Oh no. I mean yes. Yes! I'd like an audience," Dana said breathlessly, not at all sure if she was doing the right thing. "Let's go." She led the way down the red-carpeted hall, her cello rolling by her side. "OK . . . this room should be free," Dana muttered. She opened the doors to the small, intimate practice room and flipped on the lights. "You can sit over there." She indicated the one comfortable upholstered chair in the room.

What now? Dana glanced at Todd as she set up her music. He appeared completely relaxed as he sat with his long legs stretched in front of him and an expectant expression on his face. *Well, I'm glad* he's *relaxed,* she thought as butterflies swirled in her stomach.

Dana sat down on her metal chair and arranged the folds of her sapphire silk skirt around her. She pushed up the sleeves of her creamy angora sweater and did some limbering exercises with her hands. She positioned her cello and took out her bow. Pausing for an instant, she took a deep breath and tried hard to forget the nightmare of her last practice session. She found her center of concentration, tapped out the tempo in her head, and drew the bow across her strings.

The sound that filled the room was pure gold.

Dana raised her eyes heavenward and offered a silent prayer. The music flowed out of her effortlessly. It was a delight to play, and Dana threw herself wholeheartedly into the music. She could see out of the corner of her eye that Todd was staring at her in awe. But that was the only thought that penetrated her consciousness. Every fiber of her being was invested in her work. Her fingers were nimble, and the bow flew across the strings with ease. She came to the end of the piece, attacking the crescendo with abandon. The last notes lingered in the air like a fragrant memory as Dana put down her bow.

Todd leaped to his feet in a one-man standing ovation.

"Stop!" Dana couldn't help blushing, but she was pleased and touched by Todd's reaction.

"You're a genius!" Todd said. It was obvious that he was being sincere. "Bravo! Bravo!"

Dana waved the compliment away with her hand. She couldn't believe how well she'd just played. Those limbering exercises must have really helped a lot, and getting back on her practice schedule had clearly done wonders for her discipline.

She smiled. *Maybe it's the limbering exercises, maybe it's my discipline—or maybe,* Dana thought, *just maybe, it's the company.*

"Nick, Nick, wait up!" Jessica cried breathlessly. She flung herself at him just as he turned a corner and managed to grab the sleeve of his leather jacket.

"Nick," Jessica sobbed. She fell into his arms. "I've found you. I knew I'd find you. It's been so long!" She buried her head against his chest, laughing through her tears. She was back with her lover, and nothing had ever felt so good.

Nick held her to him for a brief second, then

released her and held her at arm's length. "Do I know you?" he asked.

"I—what?" Jessica stared in horror at the pleasant-looking, green-eyed stranger who was gripping her by the shoulders. Where had Nick gone? Did he vaporize? Was this a hit man who had been sent to impersonate him so she could be captured and killed?

Jessica backed away from the leather-jacketed imposter in terror. Stumbling, she fell into the arms of another man. She felt almost paralyzed by fear, but she managed to fling her arms in front of her face and scream.

"Do I know you?" the second stranger echoed.

Jessica wheeled away from him, his voice reverberating in her head, and she covered her ears to block out the sound.

"Can I help you?" He reached out to her.

"No!" Jessica shrieked. She could see the unmistakable signs of uncontrolled lust lurking in his eyes. *He wants me!* she thought, panic-stricken. *He's after me and he wants me!*

Jessica spun away and stumbled across the quad as fast as her shaking legs would carry her. "I need to cut my hair off," she babbled. "I need to dress uglier. I can't have other men wanting me. I belong to Nick." The tears ran unchecked down Jessica's face. "I have to make myself ugly. I have to make myself ugly."

Sobbing, Jessica ran toward Dickenson. She felt as if she were being pursued by demons. She was afraid to look over her shoulder for fear of what she might see behind her. Jessica was sure that she could hear footsteps following her, and she quickened her pace.

"Jessica!" Her name floated on the wind. "Jessica, wait up!"

Jessica ran even faster, but she twisted her ankle and went sprawling. A pair of leather boots appeared in her line of vision. Jessica held her breath, waiting to see if a sawed-off shotgun would follow suit.

The boots crouched down and a pair of custom-tailored jeans, then a cashmere sweater, came into view. Jessica blinked as the concerned face of Lila Fowler floated in front of her.

"Jessica, you've got to get ahold of yourself— do you hear me?" Lila helped her to her feet. "You've got to take care of yourself. You've got to get over Nick. You've got to *move on*."

Jessica stared at her friend in disbelief. "Get over Nick?" she whispered. "Don't you understand? I'll never get over Nick."

"Jessica," Lila persisted. "You *have* to."

"I don't *have* to do anything," Jessica declared, pulling herself roughly from Lila's grasp and walking away. She had no friends. Not even her own twin sister seemed to understand her. From now on, she was completely on her own.

Chapter Ten

"Do you want to split the layer cake? Or should we each just get a raspberry tart?" Nina asked as she looked at the menu. She and Elizabeth were sitting in their favorite off-campus café, Le Monde, and it was a rule that they never had lunch there without having at least one sinful dessert.

"I have to say, layer cake sounds pretty good right now." Elizabeth flipped her ponytail over her shoulder, closed her menu, and craned her neck in search of the blackboard. "What's the Thursday special?" she asked.

"Frozen yogurt and carob chips."

Elizabeth wrinkled her nose and leaned forward, resting her elbows on the green marble table. "Look, Nina, let's forget about dessert for a second and get to the real issue. Did you see my article today?" Her eyes danced mischievously.

"Did I see it?" Nina asked as she signaled the waitress. "Girl, I think that article is going to be the talk of the campus for the next couple of weeks." She handed the waitress their menus and requested the layer cake.

"Well, what did you think?" Elizabeth persisted. "I have to tell you, I felt a little nervous writing it. It's one thing for you and me to talk about sex, but it's another to plaster my feelings all over the front page." She smiled at the waitress as she deposited a luscious-looking slice of cake in front of them. "Well, OK, the *third* page," she amended.

"I think you're really brave." Nina took a large forkful of the cake and licked some extra icing off her finger. "It takes a lot of courage to write an article on sexual ethics."

"Well, Ed assigned me the topic," Elizabeth admitted as she took a bite of the cake. "But I put that spin on it. You wouldn't believe this one guy I interviewed, Nina. He pretty much came out and admitted that he dumped this girl he really cared about because she wouldn't sleep with him!" Elizabeth laid down her fork in dismay. "I just think it's time that people heard the other side of the story, you know?" She fiddled with a yellow rose in the bud vase in the center of the table.

"I was impressed by it." Nina took a sip of her

lemonade. "I think you really laid it on the line, especially the part where you talked about how it takes an even greater commitment for some couples *not* to sleep together."

Elizabeth nodded. "I think men on this campus are spoiled." She gestured with her fork for emphasis. "They think that sex is a matter of course." *Like Tom,* she thought unhappily as his face flashed before her. "They think that girls should sleep with them just because they're in college!" *Like Todd,* she thought as she remembered seeing Lauren Hill coming out of his bathroom clad only in his basketball jersey. All of a sudden the rich dessert turned to sawdust in her mouth and she pushed the plate toward Nina. "You finish it," she said hollowly.

Nina needed no encouragement, and she dug into the cake with gusto. Elizabeth pleated her pink linen napkin unhappily as she watched her friend. "Nina," she said suddenly. "Are you glad that you and Bryan took things slow? Or do you feel like you're really missing something?"

"Both," Nina admitted as she scraped the last flakes of chocolate from the plate. "I'd love to know what it *feels* like, but at the same time I figure that I can always take that step. Besides—" She pushed away the plate and looked at Elizabeth frankly. "I don't know that I can really trust Bryan that much. I mean, there are so many girls after him—sometimes it's hard for me to believe he really wants me. Just the other day I found some girl's name scrawled all over his notebook. . . ." Nina trailed off unhappily.

"That makes me sick." Elizabeth shook her head. "Why would Bryan fool around when he has you? Why is sex with some stranger more important than companionship with the woman he loves?" She threw her napkin on the table in disgust.

"Whoa!" Nina held up her hand. "Is this Elizabeth Wakefield, the journalist who always checks her facts three times before going to print? Don't you think that you're jumping to conclusions? I said that Bryan had some woman's name scribbled in his margins, *not* that he had a harem on the side!"

"Well, OK," Elizabeth relented. "You're right. I did jump to conclusions. But Nina, you have to admit that it doesn't sound good."

What am I doing? she asked herself. She didn't want to make Nina miserable. How did *she* know what Bryan's notes meant? Her emotions were getting out of control, and she was *totally* losing her objectivity.

"Nina," Elizabeth said quietly. "I was out of line. Really. I don't know what I'm talking about."

"It's OK," Nina said shortly. She slung her backpack over her shoulder. "I'll get the check this time." She picked up the bill and brought it over to the register.

Great, Elizabeth thought, burying her head in her hands. Yet *another* fine example of how sex could screw everything up.

Tom sat back in his office chair and reached out a hand for the mail that covered his old, battle-scarred desk. He loved reading junk mail and always opened the envelopes that announced he was an instant winner. Today, however, his mind was on other things, and he swept most of the mail into the garbage without even looking at it.

Tom cast a guilty look at the door to make sure that it was closed. He loved to read the *Gazette* first thing every morning, but he didn't necessarily want his colleagues at WSVU to know that.

He opened the freshly printed paper and scanned the table of contents for Elizabeth's byline. Ever since he'd seen her running toward the *Gazette* offices, he'd been eaten alive with curiosity to know what she'd been working on. Tom saw that her new article appeared on page three, and he eagerly flipped to it.

"I don't believe it," he muttered, his jaw dropping in amazement as he took in the headline.

"'Sexual Ethics? A Return to Morality'? Who died and left you Princess Grace, Elizabeth Wakefield?"

Tom hunched forward with his elbows on the desk and devoured the article. An angry frown twisted his features as the gist of Elizabeth's piece sank in. He couldn't believe she was carrying on about *virginity* as if it were the Holy Grail. "God, get over yourself," Tom grumbled. He resisted the urge to crumple the paper up and throw it away. Instead he read on with sick fascination.

Is she talking about me? he wondered as he read about "John," a guy who dumped the woman he loved just so he could sleep with someone he didn't. Tom glanced furtively over his shoulder. He half expected the WSVU staffers to be standing behind him, laughing and pointing fingers.

Tom banged his fist down on the desk. Why should he be embarrassed? There was nothing wrong with what he did. It was just Elizabeth and her mind games, screwing up his thoughts again. He pushed back his chair and began pacing angrily up and down the room.

Some people might even say that Elizabeth's the one who should be embarrassed, he mused, punching the air with his fist for emphasis. *What college-age woman who insists she's madly in love with her boyfriend doesn't have sex with him?* Last time he checked, it wasn't the sixteenth century anymore.

Tom flung himself down on his old office couch with a self-righteous expression on his face. "So, Elizabeth Wakefield, *serious* investigative reporter, announces to the world how she feels about *virginity*," Tom sneered. "Big deal. She's not the only one who has ideas about sex. And she's not the only one who has a *forum* for her ideas about sex." Tom sat up with a small smile, an idea dawning in his mind. His writer's block was now officially over and done.

Tom chortled as he ran over to his desk and grabbed a yellow legal pad.

"Now, what should I call this piece? 'Sexual Ethics: A Rebuttal'? Or how about, 'Bitter, Uptight Virgins and the Men They Don't Love Enough'?" Tom couldn't help chuckling. "Man, just *wait* until Elizabeth sees this one air. It'll probably be the biggest shock to her since she found out there wasn't a Santa Claus."

Jessica sat in the back of a cab as it rattled down the streets of Sweet Valley. She was on her way to visit Isabella at the hospital, and she didn't feel up to taking the bus.

Jessica didn't really *want* to visit Isabella in the hospital. She *wanted* to stay at home and stare at the walls. But she knew she should make an effort to do something, and visiting Isabella seemed like a safer bet than wandering around campus. Besides, she felt guilty about not seeing Isabella for so long. Isabella probably thought she'd forgotten all about her.

"Here we are," the driver said as he pulled up at the main entrance to Sweet Valley Memorial.

Jessica paid and stepped gingerly out of the cab. She was a little nervous about going into the hospital. Hospitals made her think of ambulances, and ambulances made her think of Nick. She closed her eyes tightly as an image of a body bag being loaded on a stretcher into an ambulance flashed before her.

Don't think about that now, Jessica told herself, choking back a sob as she walked up the stairs and into the lobby. The antiseptic smell depressed her and the frantic atmosphere, with doctors running to and fro, was somewhat frightening, but she managed to find her way to the information desk.

"I'd like Miss Ricci's room. That's Isabella Ricci. Could you tell me where that is?" Jessica asked a harried-looking nurse who was busy going over some charts.

The nurse put down her charts and went over to the computer. "I'm sorry," she said as she scanned up and down the screen. "There's no Isabella Ricci here."

"But that's impossible," Jessica spluttered. "She has to be here."

The nurse shook her head. "Sorry, I don't . . . oh, here it is. She's been discharged. She's staying at the Stanhope Towers."

That must mean she's better! Jessica realized. She actually felt something resembling happiness for the first time in ages. At least *one* of them was doing well.

"Thank you." Jessica left the information desk and went out into the sunlight again. She grabbed the first cab she saw and settled back against the upholstered seat as the cabbie drove her toward the Stanhope. She hoped Isabella had a fabulous suite. Then they could order room service and rent movies. Jessica felt the mildest flicker of excitement at the thought. It was only a flicker, but it was the most she'd had in a very long time.

She got out of the cab and walked through the ornate lobby to reception, where a bellboy immediately whisked Jessica toward the mahogany-and-brass elevators. *I could sure use some of this,* Jessica thought as she got off the elevator on Isabella's floor.

"Hello?" Jessica knocked on the door of the Riccis' suite. "Anybody home?"

"Hello," Mrs. Ricci said as she answered the door. "You must be Jessica. I've seen your

161

picture. Why don't you come and say hello to Isabella? She's resting in bed, but you can stay for a few minutes. I'll be in the other room if you need anything."

"Hey, Izzy," Jessica said softly as she walked through the awesome suite. She could see that Isabella was resting on a mountain of pillows in a king-size bed and that her head was turned away from Jessica. "Iz! How are you?" Jessica walked around to the other side of the bed and smiled at her friend.

Isabella frowned at her.

Was she angry at her for not visiting more? Jessica felt a twinge of guilt, and she moved forward to take Isabella's hand.

"Who are you?" Isabella asked fretfully.

"Izzy." Jessica stopped dead in her tracks. "It's me, Jessica! Don't you know who I am?"

Isabella shrugged and turned away her head.

"Izzy," Jessica begged. "Don't you know me? Izzy, please! Don't do this to me! I need to talk to you." Jessica began to cry. Her slim shoulders shook with the force of her sobs. "Oh, Izzy, do you know that Nick's dead? He's gone, and so am I. Is that why you don't recognize me? Because I've changed so much without him? I know I'm not beautiful anymore," Jessica rambled, and her words were barely audible. "I know I'm not special anymore without him. . . . Maybe I don't even know who I *am* without him." Jessica wept inconsolably.

Isabella kept her head turned. "Why are you telling me all this?" she asked. "I don't even know who you are."

"I know that's why you don't recognize me," Jessica gasped out. "Because I'm not even *me* anymore! I'm not even me anymore," she repeated. Then she ran out of the suite and out of the hotel.

Now that's *a good-looking guy!* Dana stared at the athlete's sweat-slicked, muscular body as he leaped through the air with the grace of a gazelle. The basketball went cleanly through the hoop with a small whooshing sound, and Dana had to resist the urge to clap.

Todd! She gasped as the guy jogged toward the metal fence to grab his towel. Dana was mesmerized by his lean, sculpted muscles that were covered by smooth, bronzed skin. She swallowed hard. Why didn't anyone ever tell her he looked that good without a shirt on?

"Hey, Dana!" Todd called. "I didn't see you. What brings you over this way?"

"Oh . . . I don't know." Dana blushed slightly. "Sometimes it's hard to wheel this through the quad." She gestured toward her bulky cello case. "There are so many students running around. I thought it would be easier if I took a detour near the basketball courts." No lie there. She *did* often take the long way around in order to avoid the crush of people. But she also knew that some part of her had been secretly hoping she'd run into Todd.

"I'm glad you did." Todd grinned. "I was about to take a break and grab some lunch. Want to join me?"

Dana nodded mutely as she watched Todd towel off his arms. His biceps were the best thing that she'd seen in weeks.

"OK, I'm just going to jump in the shower. I'll be back in a few." Todd turned and sprinted toward the locker rooms.

"You have *got* to stop drooling over that boy," Dana told herself as she leaned against the wire fence that enclosed the basketball court. She shifted gently to avoid snagging her cream-colored cashmere sweater on the wire and smoothed down her wine-colored suede pants. "You're finally getting your music under control. Let's not muddy the waters, OK?"

"Ready?" Todd called as he bounded over to her. He shook his head, and water droplets went flying as if he were a wet puppy dog.

"Ready," Dana said, and she fell into step beside him. "Do you want to go to the student union or the Red Lion?"

"Hmmm . . . how about the Red Lion? I'm in the mood for their chili-dusted onion rings."

Todd skipped sideways a little to avoid slamming into Dana's cello as she wheeled it between them.

"Sorry." Dana twitched the cello strap. "The Red Lion sounds great." She smiled at Todd as they made their way over to the café, but his nearness was affecting her uncomfortably. The more she thought about it, the more she realized that "running into" him had been a bad idea.

Chapter
Eleven

"After you," Todd said as he opened the door to the restaurant. Dana walked in and parked her cello near the coat stand.

"I'll just have a salad." Dana waved away the menu as she slid into the booth across from Todd.

"Onion rings, a cheeseburger—medium rare—and a Coke," Todd ordered. "So." He leaned back and spread his red-and-white-checked napkin on his lap. "How did it go today?" He nodded toward Dana's cello.

"What? Oh, fine." Dana busied herself with rearranging the salt and pepper shakers.

"That's good." Todd nodded in approval. "My practice went pretty well today too."

"Good." Dana tried to sound enthusiastic, but the easy banter that she'd been able to share with Todd over the past few days seemed to be evaporating in a swirl of nervousness. *Get a grip, girl,* Dana scolded herself. *You're having lunch with a buddy—no biggie. Stop acting like a school-girl!*

"Dana?" Todd frowned slightly as he took a sip of the large Coke the waitress had placed at his elbow. "Is something wrong?"

"No." Dana shook her head decisively, picked up her fork, and toyed with her salad. "Things are fine." She played with her napkin nervously. "I had a great prac . . . Todd." Dana put down her fork and looked him straight in the eye. "Did you read the article in the *Gazette*?" she blurted out.

"The *Gazette*?" Todd's gaze was shuttered. "I don't think I . . ." He put down his burger and smiled sheepishly. "Elizabeth's article? The one on sexual ethics? Yeah, I read it, all right."

"It made me feel like such a loser," Dana confessed. "Worse than a loser. Like . . . like some evil temptress. Did you read the part about men who love one woman but sleep with another? I felt like she was writing about me and Tom. Correction—I felt like she was talking about me, Tom, *and* herself, the whole sorry triangle." Dana blushed a fiery red and lowered her eyes. She couldn't believe what she'd just admitted to Todd, but she couldn't stop herself either.

Todd reached over and tapped her hand gently. "Hey. You can talk to me about it if you want."

"Thanks." Dana composed herself. "I mean . . ." She gestured with her hands. "She came off as so lily-white, and I feel like such damaged goods. I know Tom didn't love me, and we *did* sleep together." She turned her face away from Todd altogether as she continued speaking. "What does that make him? What does that make *me?*" Tears welled up in Dana's eyes, and she held her napkin to her face. "*Am* I just damaged goods now?" she whispered. "Do I have a red letter *A* painted on my chest? Was I so bad? Was I so wicked?"

Her shoulders began to shake as she cried in earnest. Soon her napkin was soaked through with her tears, and she flung it down on the table. Todd pressed his own into her hands and held on for a brief second. His touch was warm and reassuring, and Dana forced herself to look at him again.

"Do you know how hard it is for me to sit here with you?" she continued, her voice barely audible. "Do you know how hard it is for me to know that you once loved her? Maybe still do? That people are walking around on this campus saying that I have some obsession with Elizabeth Wakefield's men? Oh, Todd, what *am* I?"

Todd smiled, and his brown eyes were soft and caring. "You're a beautiful, talented, healthy young woman who has normal desires, and . . . like the rest of us . . . sometimes makes the wrong decisions." Todd's voice was husky, and he increased the pressure on her hand. "Who's to say that you even made the wrong choice? Maybe it was right for you to get so heavily involved with Tom. Maybe *he* made the wrong choice when he went back to Elizabeth. It doesn't look like *that's* working out too well."

"You don't think I'm damaged goods?" Dana asked quietly.

"For what? Not going to the altar 'pure'?" Todd snorted. "Give me a break. Do you think I'm damaged goods? I'm not a virgin either, and just like . . . a lot of people, I slept with someone I *wasn't* in love with. And I did it while I was on the outs with Elizabeth. Just how do you think the article made *me* feel?"

Dana's eyes widened in stunned surprise. "I didn't know that about you and Elizabeth. Oh, I know that you went out, but . . ." Dana dried her eyes and looked at Todd curiously. "How *did* the article make you feel?"

"Terrible!" Todd exclaimed. "Like I was some moral degenerate! And you know what? I *did* lose my virginity to the wrong person. But I hurt myself just as much as I hurt Elizabeth." Todd paused and took a deep breath, but he still kept a firm grip on Dana's hand. "What do you think college is about?" he continued. "It's not just

170

about books and courses and ideas. It's also about relationships. It's about finding out who you are and how you deal with people. It's about moving to the next level, and sometimes that means sex."

"Who did you sleep with?" Dana stared at him in fascination. She'd never had a conversation like this with a guy before.

"Her name was Lauren Hill—we didn't last very long. Truthfully, it happened for all the wrong reasons." Todd sighed. "Elizabeth wouldn't sleep with me, I pressured her, we broke up, I went somewhere else. End of story."

"Do you miss Elizabeth?" Dana's heart thumped against her ribs.

"No," Todd said decisively. "The fact is, I think we were headed for a breakup anyway. We did get back together for a little while, and it just didn't work. You see, Dana"—his eyes bored into hers intensely—"I don't think sex is really all there is to a relationship. If that's why a couple is breaking up, then I think there are other issues. Gin-Yung and I, we never slept together. . . ." Todd trailed off. "What I do know is, don't listen to me." He picked up an onion ring and took a bite. "The only thing that I know for certain is that sex sure has a way of screwing up relationships."

Dana burst into laughter, Todd joined in,

and soon the whole coffee shop was staring at them in amazement.

"I guess that's one way of putting it." Dana giggled. She glanced away from Todd again. This time it wasn't out of shame, but because she was afraid to reveal to him the feelings that she knew were blazing out of her eyes.

Danny whistled a cheerful tune as he entered the hotel lobby and strolled across the Persian carpet toward the elevators. Things were finally starting to look up.

He smiled at his reflection in the polished brass doors. As far as Danny was concerned, the Theta tea had been an unqualified success. Of course Isabella still hadn't regained her memory, and she still didn't seem to know who he was most of the time, but there was no denying that she'd thawed considerably toward him.

She looked at me like she could trust me, Danny remembered happily as he plucked a rose from one of the massive arrangements and threaded it through his buttonhole. *She looked at me like she could fall in love with me all over again.* He knew that was a long way from recovery, but he couldn't help feeling optimistic. Danny was sure that a love like theirs would prevail.

Danny stepped into the mahogany-lined elevator and punched the sixth-floor button. He could barely contain his excitement at the thought of seeing Isabella again. Maybe the Riccis would decide to let them take a romantic stroll on the beach. Danny liked Isabella's parents OK, but he had to admit that it would be nice to be alone with her for a change.

Danny got out on the sixth floor and practically danced down the hall toward the Riccis' suite. He was surprised to see that the door was slightly ajar, but his heart fairly leaped out of his chest when he saw that a bellboy was busy carrying out luggage.

Isabella's coming back to school! Danny thought joyfully. He raced into the room with a mile-wide smile plastered on his face. Isabella sat near the window while her mother attended to some last-minute details.

"Izzy!" Danny ran to her.

"Hello, Danny." Mrs. Ricci blocked his way. She was dressed for traveling and had a silk jacket draped over her arm.

"Mrs. Ricci, hi! I'm so happy that you're bringing Isabella back to campus," Danny said enthusiastically. "I knew that the Theta tea would help. I mean, I know it didn't quite jog her memory, but we did seem to establish a new level of trust." He made an effort to get past Mrs. Ricci, but she continued to block his way.

"We're not taking Isabella back to school,

Danny." Mr. Ricci came into the room. He was carrying three passports, and Danny spotted some airline tickets tucked discreetly among a pile of travel brochures. "We're taking Isabella to Switzerland, and we're leaving today. I've just been on the phone with Dr. Soames—he's an internationally known expert in these matters, and he thinks we don't have time to delay." Mr. Ricci stuffed some traveler's checks into a folder. "I'm sorry, Danny, but we've been too permissive. Staying here is only hurting Isabella."

This can't be happening, Danny thought as he looked at Mrs. Ricci for confirmation. *This must be a dream. It isn't real.* He closed his eyes as if the action might make the reality disappear. But when he opened them and saw the Riccis leading Isabella away, he knew he wasn't dreaming. In fact, the nightmare was just beginning.

Nina hugged her heavy physics textbook to her chest as she walked slowly across campus toward the labs. A frown marred her face as her conversation with Elizabeth replayed itself in her mind.

Just because Bryan has some woman's name written all over his notebook does not mean he's sleeping with every woman on this campus, she told herself with considerably more confidence than she felt. Elizabeth had just jumped to conclusions because of her own bad experiences with men. Nina should have felt bad *for* her. She shouldn't have been mad *at* her.

"Hey, Bryan," Nina called as she walked into the lab. She tried to make her voice sound cheery, but there was no denying that she was nervous. She shrugged out of her plum-colored cardigan and reached for her white lab coat.

"Hey, Nina, what's happening?" Bryan flashed her one of his dazzling smiles.

Why don't you tell me? Nina thought sourly, but she pushed the thought out of her mind and returned his smile.

"Not much." She reached for a beaker and flipped open her textbook.

"So how's that extra-credit project going?" Bryan frowned as he carefully added a chemical to the solution he was preparing.

"I haven't started it yet," Nina replied shortly. She didn't look up from what she was doing, and she could tell that Bryan was surprised by how abrupt she was being. *Maybe Maria is nicer to him than I am,* she thought with a twinge of anxiety. "How's yours?" she asked, making an effort to sound extra sweet. "Didn't you mention at the restaurant the other day that you were thinking of doing one yourself?"

"Did I?" Bryan averted his eyes. "I don't

remember." He busied himself with weighing some sodium hydroxide.

What's going on here? Nina wondered unhappily. *I know he told me about a project. Is he doing it with Maria? Is that why he won't tell me about it?*

"Bryan." Nina wheeled around suddenly to face him. "Who's Maria?" she demanded, her heart thudding against her ribs.

"Huh? I don't know what you're talking about." Bryan looked bewildered, but Nina was sure that she could see a telltale blush spreading itself across his cheeks.

"Maria," she persisted. "You had her name written all over your notebook, Bryan. I saw it." *Go on,* Nina urged him mentally. *Clap your hand to your forehead and say, "Oh, that Maria! She's my maiden aunt, and I have to remember to get her a ninetieth birthday present."*

But Bryan did no such thing. He simply shrugged and went back to his measuring.

"Bryan," Nina said softly. "Is something wrong?"

"Of course not," Bryan said heartily, but he refused to look Nina in the eye. "What could possibly be wrong?"

I don't know, Nina thought sadly. *But something definitely is.*

"This is fine—over here on the right." Jessica reached into her purse and shoved a bill at the

176

driver, not even bothering to see what denomination it was.

"Hey, lady." The cabdriver twisted around, concern written on his features. "You're sure this is what you want? The cemetery? Maybe I could drive you somewhere else. It looks like it's about to rain. You should get yourself inside. Don't you have some friends you'd like to visit?"

"Already tried that one," Jessica said, barking out a laugh. "Didn't work out too well. Don't worry," she assured the driver in a steely voice. "This is where I belong."

Jessica flung open the cab door. The wind whipped her hair into a tangle as she staggered out. She made it across the street and struggled with the latch on the wrought-iron gate that led to the small cemetery. The gate creaked open, and Jessica hurled herself through it. She stumbled, her heels catching in the mud, and fell on all fours, scraping her knees painfully on some small pebbles. She collapsed into the muck and considered staying there for the rest of her life.

"No. I have to get up," she whispered. "I have to see Nick's grave." Jessica pushed herself to a kneeling position. "I have to get up," she repeated like a mantra. But the effort was too much for her, and she fell back down again.

"No. No. I have to see Nick," Jessica told

herself. Her shoulders shook, and her tears mixed with the dirt on her face to form muddy rivers that streamed down her cheeks. "I have to get there. I don't care if I have to crawl a thousand miles over broken glass."

She dragged herself slowly and painfully through the maze of tombstones until she came to Nick's grave site.

"Nick, Nick, *please* come back to me," Jessica cried. Her slim body was racked with sobs, and she pulled at her hair as she rocked back and forth against Nick's tombstone.

Her words died on the wind, which howled around her. True to the cabbie's prediction, a storm was rising. Rain fell in huge, stinging drops, and streaks of lightning tore through the sky.

"Nick, how could you leave me like this?" Jessica repeated over and over, her voice competing with the rising thunder. "Come back to me, please!"

Jessica traced the letters on his tombstone as tenderly as if they were a part of Nick himself. "Oh, Nick," she whispered. "I can't go on without you. I want to be where you are now." She kissed the tips of her fingers, then touched them to the headstone. With a deep shudder she threw herself down on the grave.

The cold, wet dirt chilled Jessica to the bone, and the rain hammered down on her in torrential sheets. She lifted her head and shook her fists at the sky, furious at the forces that robbed her of her lover.

As she laid her head back down on the grave, she imagined that she was resting on Nick's muscular chest. Her arms hugged the muddy ground and her fingers dug into the dirt as if she could bury herself along with him.

The effort proved too much for her, and she lay spent, her muscles screaming with pain and her mind dissolving in agony.

Jessica lay completely still as the storm grew. She was oblivious to the world around her. The rain that pelted her so savagely might as well have been a gentle breeze, and the flashing electricity that rent the sky could have been a rainbow for all she cared.

"Nick?" Jessica whispered. She shifted slightly on the hard ground. Although she knew that Nick was beyond her, she seemed to feel a strange connection to him. His spirit seemed to waft up from beneath the earth and fill the air around her.

"Nick?" Jessica looked around her, half expecting to see a wraithlike vision floating in front of her. She could feel his strength like an electric force that vibrated through the atmosphere. It seemed to seep into her bones and curl itself around her insides, where it warmed her, taking away some of the pain of the last few weeks.

Jessica wiped the tears from her eyes and sat up slowly. Although her face was muddied and her hair completely disheveled, Jessica suddenly looked—and felt—more together than she had in days. Her eyes had some of their old fire back, and her posture was ramrod straight.

"I've been so lonely without you, Nick," Jessica said quietly. "Everything is falling apart without you. I've let *myself* fall apart." She hung her head in shame. "I owe it to our love to stay strong." Jessica gasped as the realization hit her full force.

"I have to keep going." She sprang to her feet with newfound strength. "I have to, as a testament to our love. If I don't, it will be like we both were killed." Jessica faltered on the words. Part of her still wished that she were dead. Life without Nick was unutterably painful, but she knew now that to give in to her grief was ultimately to give in to injustice. If she let her life be destroyed, then all Nick's work and his tragic death would be for nothing.

"I can't make Nick come back," Jessica murmured sadly. The words seared through her, leaving a swath of raw pain. "But I can make sure that I live my life in a way that he would be proud of."

Jessica smoothed back her wet hair and squared

her shoulders. "I promise you, Nick, that I will strive to be the kind of woman that you would have admired. I'll always love you, and I'll always miss you, but I'll learn to go on." The thunder underscored her words as she stood stock-still and stared toward the sky.

"I'll learn to go on," Jessica repeated quietly. She bowed her head in silent prayer for a moment. "All right, my love," she whispered. "Good-bye."

Jessica strode from the cemetery. Her heart was heavy, but her feet grew lighter with every step.

Chapter Twelve

"Psst! Hey, Elizabeth."

Elizabeth looked up in surprise. Nina was smiling at her sheepishly over the top of the study carrel. She came over and knelt beside Elizabeth. "Are you busy?"

"Not really," Elizabeth whispered back. She was aware that the other students in the library's rare-book room were staring at them. "I'm just finishing up some overdue work for Professor Young. . . . I had to check some obscure sources." She held up an ancient, leather-bound volume. "What's up?"

"Let's go talk in the lounge for a sec, OK?" Nina's eyes were pleading. She gestured toward the other students, who were already making shushing noises. "I'm not really in the mood to get a lot of dirty looks right now."

Elizabeth gathered her things and followed Nina down the green-carpeted library hallway to the lounge. She was in need of a break, and she was glad that Nina had shown up, but she couldn't help wondering if her faux pas at lunchtime was forgotten or not.

"Listen, Nina, about lunch . . . I didn't mean what I said," Elizabeth offered as she sat down in one of the dark red leather chairs in the lounge.

"Forget it." Nina sat down across from Elizabeth and put her books on the round, burled-walnut table that separated them. "I was being too sensitive. In fact"—she paused and gave a grim smile—"you may be right."

"About Bryan sleeping around?" Elizabeth's eyes widened in surprise. Disgusting! First Tom, now Bryan . . . was it contagious?

"No." Nina shook her head. "I don't think that he's really sleeping around, but *something's* weird between us. I just can't figure out what."

"I'm really sorry, Nina." Elizabeth stretched her denim-clad legs out in front of her. "I'm not going to go off like I did at lunch and insist that he *has* to be sleeping around. But let's face it— men can be really awful." She sighed and wrapped her pink-flowered cardigan tightly around her.

"I know," Nina replied soberly. She leaned forward and rested her elbows on the table. "I tried confronting him about the name in his notebook, but he acted like he didn't know what I was talking about. Somehow that made things even worse."

"I know what you mean," Elizabeth said sympathetically. "It's like with me and Tom. It wasn't bad enough that he slept with Dana . . . he had to *lie* about it too." She jumped up and began pacing restlessly back and forth on the multicolored carpet, her mind teeming with bitter memories.

"What do *you* think Bryan is up to?" Nina asked.

"You know what I think?" Elizabeth spun around so fast that her blond hair flew about her face in a golden swirl. "I think that you and I should stop caring so much about what men like Tom and Bryan do." She stopped pacing and rejoined Nina in front of the fire.

"Hey, aren't the Alpha Delts throwing a hot party tomorrow night?" she demanded.

"I think so." Nina's brow furrowed. "But what do you care?"

"Because . . ." Elizabeth gave Nina a small smile. "You and I are going to be there."

"We *are?*" Nina asked doubtfully.

"We are!" Elizabeth crowed. "It's about time we gave guys a taste of their own medicine. Let's stop mooning over no-goods like Bryan and Tom. They're *not* the only men in the universe."

"But we hate frat parties," Nina protested.

"You've always said that you've never had a good time at them."

That was certainly true, Elizabeth realized. Maybe a frat party wasn't such a great idea. But she'd rather be at a frat party than sitting around in her dorm room, thinking about Tom and getting shrieked at by Jessica.

"So what?" Elizabeth shrugged. "That's the past. Look, Nina, all I know is that there's a party tomorrow night." She paused dramatically. "And *we* are going to be the toast of it."

"No!" Danny yelled. He pushed his way past Mr. Ricci and flung himself at Isabella. "You can't take her away. You can't." He threw his arms around her. "I won't let you."

Isabella looked terrified at Danny's outburst, but he was sure that he could also see her love for him shining in her eyes. "I won't let them take you, Izzy," he whispered, kneeling down beside her. He stroked her hair tenderly. "I love you . . . I really do. Maybe you don't know that, and maybe you don't remember, but you used to love me too. And I promise you, I won't let them take you away."

"I'm going to have to ask you to let go of my daughter," Mr. Ricci declared, his voice stern as he advanced toward Danny. "We have a car waiting downstairs to take us to the airport, and these outbursts aren't helping anybody, least of all Isabella."

Danny ignored him completely. His entire being was focused on Isabella. "Do you want to go with them, Isabella? Do you want to go to Switzerland?"

Isabella whimpered. She looked terrified, and she clung tightly to Danny's hand. "I don't . . . I don't know. . . ."

"You see?" Danny whipped his head around and glared at Mr. Ricci. "She's scared. She doesn't want to go."

"The only thing I see is that *you're* scaring her, young man," Mr. Ricci growled. "Please move away so I don't have to use force."

Danny looked at Mrs. Ricci with his heart in his eyes. "Please, Mrs. Ricci," Danny said, tears forming at the corners of his eyes. "Don't let this happen. Let Isabella stay."

"I'm so sorry, Danny," Mrs. Ricci gasped. She gave him a watery smile. "I know how much Isabella means to you. But sometimes love isn't enough."

"No . . . ," Danny sobbed. He buried his head in Isabella's lap. His shoulders heaved, and his tears flowed. Isabella laid a tentative hand on his shoulders. Danny looked up into her calm, gray eyes. "You do love me, Isabella. You do."

But Isabella's hand was rudely jerked away as

Mr. Ricci pulled Danny to his feet. "You're forcing me to be cruel, Danny." The expression on his face was pained. "Let me do what's right for my daughter." He gestured to the bellboys to lead Isabella away. "She'll get her memory back at the sanitarium. It's the only way. And if you two are meant to be together . . ." His voice caught for a brief moment, but he controlled himself and went on. "Then she'll come back to you." He nodded to his wife, picked up his briefcase, and turned to go.

"You can't do this," Danny cried. He raced after them, but the elevator doors closed in his face.

Danny grabbed the door to the stairs and yanked it open with brute force. He tore down the stairs with superhuman speed and raced out into the parking lot just as the Riccis were loading Isabella into a waiting limousine.

"Isabella!" Danny bellowed at the top of his lungs. "Isabella! Don't go! Don't let them take you away!" But his words were drowned out by the roar of the limousine as it took off in a cloud of exhaust.

Danny sank to his knees in the parking lot and wept helplessly as the limousine sped away, taking Isabella, and all his hopes and dreams, away with it.

*　　*　　*

Jessica woke up early. She lay on her back and stared at the ceiling, just as she had every other morning since Nick had died. But this morning was different. After her experience in the graveyard yesterday, she was determined to get her life back on track. She knew that would be the most fitting tribute she could give to Nick's memory.

"Rise and shine," Jessica murmured to herself as she swung her slim legs over the edge of the bed. She winced as she saw how long it had been since she'd shaved. She'd take care of that first thing. Today she was going to look like the Jessica that Nick had known and loved, and the natural look was *not* part of that picture.

Jessica wrapped her pink silk robe around her. She grabbed one of Elizabeth's blue towels and wandered over to her dresser, where she began shoveling bath and beauty products into her quilted makeup bag. She nodded in satisfaction as she filled it to overflowing. With a smile she zipped it up, and tucking it under her arm, she opened the door and made her way to the bathroom.

Jessica had the bathroom entirely to herself. She piled her things on a chair and turned the shower on as hot as she could make it.

"Mmm, this *does* feel good," she purred as she uncapped a bottle of raspberry-scented body

189

lotion and began applying it to her hair. She was a little irritated that she couldn't work up a lather. Well, that didn't matter. It was time to apply conditioner anyway. She shot her hand out of the shower and plucked a canister of shaving cream from her supplies on the chair. Jessica rubbed the shaving cream into her scalp with abandon. Now *that* made a nice lather. She rinsed the foam from her hair, scrubbed her whole body with a twenty-dollar sea-algae facial bar, and turned off the shower.

She wrapped the blue towel around herself and approached the sink. Cheerfully she squeezed some hair gel onto her toothbrush. She brushed her teeth vigorously with the gel, barely noticing the strange taste.

"Foundation first, then a little blush," Jessica murmured as she rummaged in her beauty bag. She grabbed a bottle of self-tanner and began smoothing it on her face. What a difference a good base made. She reached back in her bag and pulled out a bright red lipstick. She unswiveled it and dabbed the color on her cheeks.

"Better and better," Jessica mused happily. She deftly filled in her lip line with some purple eyeliner and stood back to survey her handiwork.

Jessica smiled at her reflection and made a kissy face. She gathered up her things and bounded out of the bathroom, impatient to get dressed. Back in her dorm room, she flung open her closet. How about that new red-and-black plaid skirt? Nick always did love the schoolgirl look. She rifled through her many blouses, trying to find the perfect match.

"This is it!" Jessica exclaimed. She held up a purple flowered silk blouse. Jessica kicked the closet shut with her foot and hurried into her ensemble. She shoved her feet into a pair of clogs and grabbed a beaded evening purse.

"I'm ready to face the world," Jessica cried triumphantly. She opened the door and sashayed down the hall, singing a little song as she went out to greet the day.

Tom reached his arm out from under the covers and grabbed the alarm clock that was shrilling in his ear. He threw it against the wall and sighed with relief when it stopped ringing.

I'm not getting out of bed today, he vowed. Why would he want to do anything that stupid? Who knew what the day held in store for him. Another article about sexual ethics by his ex-girlfriend? Dana running around in a daze, like she'd finally found true love?

"Rise and shine, Tombo." Danny's voice floated across the room. He sounded about as happy as Tom felt.

"What's wrong with *you*?" Tom turned to

look at his roommate, and his jaw dropped in shock. Danny looked as if he had been crying for a week.

"Gee." Danny laced his hands behind his head and pretended to consider Tom's question. "Let's see, could it be that the love of my life was forced out of the country by her parents yesterday? Nah . . . it's probably that they were out of ice cream at the cafeteria last night."

"Isabella's gone? Oh, man, I'm really sorry." Tom sat up in bed and hugged his knees. "I thought my problems were bad." He laughed bitterly and wrapped his striped blanket more closely around him. "Where is Isabella?" he asked quietly.

Danny turned to look at him. "Halfway around the world by now, I'd guess." He shrugged, his mouth tightening in a grim line. "Some fancy sanitarium in Switzerland."

Tom was silent. His own problems were petty by comparison. Was there something he could do to help out? Tom racked his brains, but he couldn't come up with any brilliant ideas. "Maybe you and I need to put the whole relationship scene on hold for a while," Tom suggested.

"It already *is* on hold for me." Danny smirked unpleasantly. "The Riccis made sure of that."

"No . . . I mean we should just forget the whole thing. Go out and have a good time." Tom leaned forward as he warmed to his theme. "Isn't there a party at Alpha Delt tonight?"

Danny shrugged. It was clear that his thoughts were elsewhere. "So?" he asked dully.

"Let's hit it." Tom leaped out of bed and went over to his dresser. "Let's go and have a wild time, dude. You and me. What have we got to lose? We'll dance with some pretty girls, kick back a few drinks. Who knows, maybe we'll even have an OK time." Tom yanked open his top drawer and pulled out a T-shirt and a pair of jeans.

"Does this mean Wildman Watts is back?" Danny quirked an eyebrow.

Tom looked at himself in the mirror as he combed his hair. "No. It just means that you and I have some serious problems with the female species. I have a feeling that an Alpha Delt party might be just the cure."

Dana applied a second coat of ravishing red to her toenails, put down the polish, and grabbed the pumice stone from the small basket where she kept her beauty supplies. Since she had to keep her nails short for cello, she always made sure to take extra care with her pedicures. She finished with the pumice stone and pointed a slender ankle, the better to admire the results of her efforts.

"Someone's in a good mood," Felicity observed as she came in the living room. She dumped her backpack unceremoniously on the coffee table and plopped herself down on the couch. Her cold had disappeared, and her eyes sparkled as she teased Dana.

"Hey, watch what you're doing," Dana squealed. She lunged forward and capped the bottle of nail polish before it spilled all over the couch.

"So how come *you're* so happy?" Felicity asked. She whipped a brush out of her purse and began attacking her hair. "Not that I mind," she said hastily. "You were looking pretty down for a while."

"Was I?" Dana frowned in consideration. She jumped up from the couch and padded toward the kitchen area, careful of the cotton that separated her toes. "Want some?" She held up a can of soda for Felicity's inspection.

"Sure."

"I guess you're right. . . . I *was* bumming." She grabbed two glasses from the cabinet and popped the top of the can.

"You *guess?*" Felicity shrieked. "Dana, you were moping around here like, like . . ." She paused, as if searching for words. "Like there'd been a seventy-five-percent-off sale at Lisette's and you'd overslept! What happened?" Felicity demanded. "Because whatever it is, I want some too!"

"Dana, phone!" Cherie called from the other

room. She sauntered in, her round brown eyes wide with curiosity. "It's a guy," she stage-whispered, "and he sounds *really* cute."

Dana bounded from the room in a single leap, her pedicure forgotten, and grabbed the dangling receiver. "Hello?"

"Dana? Hi. It's me, Todd. How's it going?"

"Todd!" Dana couldn't stop the grin that overtook her face. The last time she had spoken to him was at their lunch at the Red Lion. Dana was still reeling from the intensity of their encounter.

"What's up?" She twisted the phone cord back and forth as she paced up and down the room.

"Oh, nothing much. I just felt like talking. . . ." Todd trailed off.

Although Todd's conversation was far from scintillating, Dana was fascinated by its implications. In her considerable experience, guys never called "just to talk" unless they were totally—

Whoa! she told herself. *Hold up, girl. You and Todd are just friends. He's your buddy. He doesn't think of you as anything more than that.*

Dana swallowed hard, remembering the look in his eyes as he held her hand at lunch. He was just comforting her, that was all. Nothing more . . .

"Yeah," Todd continued. "I was shooting a few baskets earlier—I had a great practice, incidentally—and I remembered that last season . . ." Todd went on about some sports scandal where a major leaguer had been thrown off the field for spitting at the umpire. At least, Dana *thought* he'd said spit. Whatever. A guy sure didn't talk about saliva with a girl he was interested in. Dana's heart sank a little at the thought.

". . . So, I was wondering if you wanted to get together again?" Todd concluded.

"What?" Dana frowned, momentarily thrown by the shift in the conversation. "Sure." *Buddy of mine,* she added silently. "There's a concert tonight that I should probably catch. It's the Mendelssohn Octet, and I want to learn the cello part."

"I'll meet you outside the student union at eight, OK? See you then."

"See you then," Dana echoed.

Dana stood lost in thought for a few minutes after they'd said their good-byes. She was meeting Todd tonight. But were they getting together as friends or as something more? Dana wasn't sure, and she wasn't sure what she wanted either.

"Who was it?" Felicity called from the living room.

"Todd," Dana said as she wandered slowly back to the couch.

"So *that's* what's put the roses in your cheeks."

Felicity raised her glass of soda in a salute. "Sounds like you're on the mend."

"It's not what you think," Dana said shortly. She ignored the questioning looks that Felicity and Cherie were exchanging.

"We're just friends," she insisted, flopping down on the couch and flipping through a fashion magazine. *It's true . . . we* are *just friends,* she realized. *Friends* talk *about sex the way Todd and I did. Lovers* do *it.*

Dana scanned the pages of the magazine, but she couldn't stop thinking about her conversation with Todd. She just didn't get it. Why did she feel so disappointed? She didn't want to get involved right now. She didn't want to be anything more than Todd's friend. Did she?

An ad for aftershave caught her eye. She studied it closely. It was hard not to notice how much better looking Todd was than the model. *Yeah, right,* she thought with an ironic laugh. *Sure, Dana, you "just want" to be friends . . . the same way Madonna "just wanted" to become a singer!*

I love you. I miss you. Come back to me, Nick, Jessica wrote in purple ink as she sat in the back row of her introductory philosophy class. She barely paid attention to what Professor Malika was saying as she scribbled frantically in her diary.

Nick, I'm trying to be the woman you want. I'll never love anyone else again.

Jessica paused and cocked her head. She was vaguely aware that the other students in the class were making a commotion. It seemed to have something to do with what the professor was saying. She put down her pen and tried to focus on his words.

"This essay is the most important project of the semester." Professor Malika paced back and forth behind the lectern, a serious expression on his face. "In fact, there will be no final exam in this class."

A few of the students whooped and cheered.

Professor Malika removed his glasses and gestured with them for emphasis. "Your grades will be solely dependent on this paper," Professor Malika explained as cheers turned to groans. "I expect to have original topics submitted to me for consideration by next period. Class over." He dismissed them with a wave of his hand.

A paper? Is that what everybody's talking about? Jessica wondered as she went back to her diary. Big deal! Who cared about a stupid paper. She began to hum a little tune to herself as she drew hearts and flowers around Nick's name.

"Ms. Wakefield?" Professor Malika called in a harsh voice. "I wonder if I might see you in my office for a second."

"OK." Jessica shrugged, scrambled to her feet, and followed him down the hall to his office.

I guess he goes in for the "existential" look, she thought as she took in the room's minimalist decor. The only chair was some strange armless contraption, the black-and-gray rug was completely threadbare, and a jungle of dying plants shed their brown leaves over everything.

Professor Malika sat down at his battered metal desk and fixed Jessica with a steely glare. "Ms. Wakefield, do you have any idea how much trouble you're in?" His muddy brown eyes gleamed cruelly behind his rimless glasses.

Who cares? Jessica shifted back and forth uncomfortably on her feet. The clogs that she was wearing were pinching her. She wished that there was someplace for her to sit. She considered asking the professor for his chair, but it looked too much like a medieval torture instrument. She sighed loudly.

"Do you find my conversation boring, Ms. Wakefield?" Professor Malika asked caustically.

Yes. Jessica fiddled with her beaded evening purse. *What does he think, that standing around a musty old office is tops on my hit parade?*

"Well." Professor Malika leaned back in his chair and crossed his arms. He wore a tweed jacket with suede elbow patches. "You may find me *boring,* Ms. Wakefield, but I find you *disgraceful.*"

Jessica was barely listening to what he was saying. She was staring at a mustard stain on one of his elbow patches. *Doesn't he know that elbow patches were out of date five years ago?* she wondered.

"You've hardly done any work all semester." Professor Malika jabbed at the air with a pencil. "You sit in the back of the room as if you're in another world," he continued, biting each word off savagely. "In fact, I doubt you've even learned the first thing about philosophy." Jessica thought that she could see foam appear at the corners of his mouth.

Yeah? OK, so? What's the problem? Jessica turned to leave.

"Ms. Wakefield!" The professor's voice was as harsh as artillery fire and twice as loud. Jessica recoiled in shock.

"You're in danger of failing the course," he explained. "Oh. Is *that* sinking in? Good. Because if you don't pull yourself together, you *will* fail. Personally, I don't think you have what it takes to make an effort," he said with a sneer. "But out of the goodness of my heart, I'm willing to give you your very own paper topic."

Fine, anything, I don't care, just get me out of here. Jessica couldn't stand being in the same room with the professor for another minute.

"I think that anarchy and death in the last

decade of the millennium might be a good subject for you to pursue." He stroked his goatee thoughtfully.

"Wha-What?" Jessica stammered.

"I said anarchy and death. You might want to read some of the German philosophers," Professor Malika droned on, unaware of the effect his words were having on Jessica.

Anarchy and death? Death? Why is death following me wherever I go? Death, dying, death . . . The words swirled through her mind like leaves blowing in the wind. She staggered out the door. She could dimly hear the professor's voice calling after her, but her mind was too full of its own ramblings to be able to listen to anyone else.

"Death." Jessica wept as she collapsed against the hard concrete wall of the corridor and sank down to the floor. "Death and dying. Death and dying. I can't take it anymore. I can't!"

Sobs racked her body, and tears blinded her eyes. She was powerless to move. For all she cared, she would stay there, stranded alone in the hallway, forever.

Danny sat up in bed, a glum expression on his face, as he watched Tom lace up his sneakers. "I don't know about this party," he muttered. "I'm not really in the mood."

"That's just it." Tom finished with his shoes

and grabbed his shaving kit from the dresser. "We're both in *miserable* moods. What better way to shake them than by going to a party?"

Danny sighed as he plucked a piece of lint off his blanket. "I don't know, Tombo. Parties have kind of bad associations for me right now." He closed his eyes briefly as an image of Isabella that fateful night flashed before him—the night that she had jumped off the balcony at the Alpha Chi house. If only he hadn't pressured her so much . . . if only she hadn't jumped . . . if only she were here with him now, the way she always had been before the accident.

Danny hung his head. He would have given anything to erase the past. He knew that wasn't possible, but that didn't stop his mind from constantly replaying the last few moments he'd spent with Isabella before he'd left her alone . . . and vulnerable. He rubbed his eyes with his fists in an attempt to block out the memory, but he couldn't stop being haunted by the anger and resentment in Isabella's face. What were those final minutes like for her? When she'd gone out of her mind on angel dust and jumped off the balcony? What could have possibly driven her to do that? Had it been him? Or had it all been a figment of her imagination?

"Forget it, Tombo. I'm just not a party animal." He averted his eyes from Tom's searching gaze.

"Feeling guilty?" Tom asked quietly.

"Yeah." Danny nodded. "I think I'll bag the party. I've got a lot to do anyway." *Yeah, like sit and stare at the walls,* he told himself. *Or how about I go really wild and watch some paint dry?*

"Look, Danny." Tom came over and clapped him on the shoulder. "You're not doing yourself any good by punishing yourself. I'm not suggesting that you morph into some party animal, but I *am* suggesting that a night out will probably make you feel a little better."

Danny shrugged, unconvinced. "I suppose I couldn't feel *worse,*" he admitted.

"Well, no one could accuse you of having the party spirit," Tom said dryly. "But can I take it that's a yes?"

"I guess so." Danny threw off the covers and got out of bed. He grabbed his shaving kit and a towel. "I'm going to hit the showers. I've got a lot of cleaning up to do."

Chapter
Thirteen

"Jessica? Jessica, are you OK?" Denise Waters knelt down beside her and tried to brush the wild tangle of hair out of her eyes.

Jessica shivered and looked at Denise in confusion. The hard, concrete floor felt as if it were seeping through her clothes and chilling her to the bone. The cinder-block wall scratched her cheek as she pillowed her head against it. All rational thought had fled her mind hours ago. *Or was it only minutes?* she wondered. She couldn't remember when she had staggered out of the professor's office. She only knew that everything since then was a blank.

Jessica wasn't quite sure who was stroking her hair so kindly. The only thing she knew was that the love and concern that flowed out of the young woman's eyes were warming and soothing her. "D-Denise?" Jessica stuttered. "Is that you?" She reached out and grasped her hand.

"It's me." Denise gave her a small smile. "Why don't you let me take you home? Do you think Elizabeth is there now?"

"No . . . I don't know where she is." She clutched Denise's hand desperately. "Please don't leave me alone, Denise. I can't take it anymore."

"Of course not," Denise said soothingly. "Let's get you over to Theta house." She helped Jessica to her feet.

"Denise, do you think that Nick still loves me?" Jessica asked brokenly as she allowed her friend to lead her out of the building. "Do you think he's somewhere in heaven, missing me?"

Denise kept a firm hand under Jessica's elbow as she led her across the quad. "I think that Nick sees you, Jessica," she said carefully. "I think he watches over you."

Jessica nodded. "I hope so. I really do. . . ." Her voice broke with fresh sobs.

"C'mon. Here we are." Denise helped Jessica up the wide steps of Theta house and into the lounge.

Jessica collapsed on the faded chintz sofa. It felt heavenly compared to the floor outside Professor Malika's office. Denise plumped up some pillows behind her head and removed her shoes.

"What's going on?" Alexandra Rollins came in from the kitchen, a steaming cup of tea in her hand. "Jessica? Are you OK?" She hurried over to the couch. "Here, honey, drink this." She offered the cup to her, and Jessica took it gratefully. She drank the tea as if it were nectar. The warm, honeyed brew soothed her aching throat, and the attention she was getting soothed her aching spirit. She was dimly aware that the room was filling up with her sorority sisters, but unlike the scene at the graveyard, this time she was thankful for their presence.

"Jessica, is there anything we can do for you?" Mandy Carmichael asked softly.

Jessica shook her head wearily. She was too spent to talk. She was simply content with lying down on the couch and being administered to.

"Well, what have we here?" Alison Quinn swept into the room.

As usual, she was dressed in a matronly ensemble that would have looked more appropriate on the Queen Mother. She sniffed disdainfully as if there were a bad smell in the air, and she looked at Jessica as if she were responsible for it.

"Jessica's not feeling well." Denise stood up and glared at Alison.

Not feeling well? Uh, can you say understatement? Jessica thought as she felt a glimmer of her spirit returning. She watched with a smirk as

Denise and Alison squared off against each other as if they were preparing for a fistfight.

"I can see that," Alison retorted, her expression pinched. "And while I understand that Jessica has been through a lot recently, I think she may be carrying the damsel-in-distress act just a little too far."

There was a shocked murmur from the rest of the Thetas, but Alison held up her hand for silence.

"The Thetas have a certain standard to uphold, and personal tragedy is no excuse for letting it slide. In fact, suffering can often ennoble one." Alison paused and gave Jessica a brutal once-over. Her eyes widened as she took in her bizarre outfit. "Regrettably, it seems to have had the opposite effect on you, Jessica. You don't appear to be Theta material at the moment, my dear."

What happened to Lady Bountiful in the graveyard? The one who promised me undying support? Jessica wondered, shaking her head. She knew that the room was expecting her to take a stand, but as much as she hated the way Alison was behaving, she just didn't have the energy to defend herself. She was glad that Denise had brought her to Theta house, and she was appreciative of the comfort her sisters offered. But beyond that, she really didn't care. She didn't care at all.

*　　　*　　　*

"So what did you think of the Mendelssohn Octet?" Dana asked as she took a small bite of her raspberry tart. She and Todd were sitting side by side in an elegant French bistro. It had been Todd's decision that they go out for dessert after the concert, and Dana had enthusiastically agreed. How could she say no when Todd looked so handsome? Besides, the music had been so fabulous and Dana was so high with excitement that she never wanted the evening to end.

"Well, to tell you the truth, I don't know that much about music, but it sounded great to me." Todd smiled affably.

"Great?" Dana exclaimed in mock horror. "It was better than great. It was way beyond awesome!" Her eyes sparkled brilliantly in the candlelight. Dana had taken special care with her hair and makeup that night. She was confident that she was having a good night beautywise, but she had no way of knowing just what effect Todd was having on her appearance. She was a woman transformed.

"It was some of the best playing I've ever heard." Dana leaned forward and adjusted the strap of her ruby satin shift. "The Huntington Quartet is world-class. They're like the . . . the . . ." Dana floundered for a second. "They're like the Shaquille Jordan of the music world." She leaned back triumphantly against the blue velvet banquette and took a sip of her espresso.

"That's *Michael* Jordan and Shaquille *O'Neal*," Todd corrected her with a chuckle. "But I get your point." He took a large bite of his Black Forest cake. "I'm glad you enjoyed it that much. When do you start learning the cello part?"

"Well." Dana reached up and wiped a dab of whipped cream from the corner of Todd's mouth with her thumb. Her whole hand tingled. "I really want to sink my teeth into it right away, but I need to get back on track with the pieces I'm already working on."

"You sounded terrific the other day," Todd offered, his voice rich with praise.

"Thank you," Dana said quietly. She nibbled on her pastry, but she couldn't take her eyes off Todd. He looked gorgeous in a dark jacket and red-and-blue-striped tie. Dana had never seen him dressed up before, and she was stunned at how sophisticated and debonair he looked.

"I mean it," Todd continued. He leaned across the small table and locked his eyes with hers. "It sounds like you got a handle on whatever was throwing you."

Maybe I do, Dana realized. *Maybe it's time I put the problems of the past behind me.*

"Remember what I said about basketball?" Todd continued. "About how sometimes your game comes back stronger after some downtime? I think that's happening with you."

"Really?" Dana was flattered. She couldn't remember the last time that a guy had put so much energy into *her* problems. She'd always played the flirt before, batting her eyelashes and sitting quietly while men poured out their hearts to her. And with Tom Watts . . .

Dana shuddered. Just getting him to forget Elizabeth at all for a stretch was a major victory. But Todd was different. He had the same commitment to his passion and the same frustrating problems with his personal "muse" as well. And best of all, he wasn't carrying a single torch for Elizabeth Wakefield. She looked at him with a new appreciation and had to fight back the urge to reach across the table and grasp his hand.

Don't forget, girl—you and Todd are just friends. Nothing more, she recited. But she couldn't help wondering, as she stared at Todd's handsome face in the flickering candlelight, whether she was once again ready to tackle more than just the cello.

Elizabeth applied a rich crimson color to her lips and stood back to admire her reflection. Although she usually didn't go in for the glamour look, tonight she had pulled out all the stops, and she had to admit that she looked pretty good. Her simple black sheath looked so-phisticated and sexy, and the tiny diamond studs that sparkled at her ears made her eyes shine even brighter.

"What do you think?" She turned to Nina, who was busy with her own makeup.

"I think you look fantastic." Nina squinted in the mirror as she applied a second coat of mas-cara. "Those shoes are fabulous." She gestured with her mascara wand at Elizabeth's strappy satin sandals. "But do I look OK?"

"You look incredible," Elizabeth said sin-cerely. Nina was dressed in a white strapless chif-fon dress that showed off her hard-fought-for figure.

"Ready to rock and roll?" Nina tilted her head questioningly.

"You bet." Elizabeth grabbed her evening purse off Nina's bed. "Let's get over to Alpha Delt."

However did Jessica manage? Elizabeth wondered as she stumbled across the grass in her high heels. She felt a brief flicker of nerves as she and Nina neared the front steps of the Alpha Delta Phi house. It had been a long time since she'd gone to a party without a date.

Nina opened the door, and they were both assaulted by a tidal wave of noise. Music blared from giant speakers, and everyone in the packed room seemed to be talking at once.

Elizabeth took a deep breath and smiled at Nina as she plunged into the crowd. She fought her way through wall-to-wall football players and over to the bar. She grabbed a cup full of something reddish and watched the scene in front of her.

"Hey, nice dress. Want to dance?" a good-looking guy asked her. Elizabeth guessed from his accent that he was an exchange student.

"No, thanks." She shook her head and gave him a small smile. The guy shrugged good-naturedly and disappeared into the crowd.

"What was I thinking?" Elizabeth cried. A little dancing with a cute guy wouldn't have done her any harm. She looked around. There were tons of good-looking men there, and none of them was Tom Watts. It was time for her to see what it was like to be with someone else. If Tom could sleep with another woman, then she could very well dance with another guy. No commitments, no regrets!

Elizabeth smiled as a big blond lug beckoned to her from the dance floor. She put down her drink and with a spring in her step went to join him.

Should I hold her hand? Todd wondered as he and Dana strolled to the bus. He looked longingly

213

at her. In the moonlight she took his breath away. Her face was cameo perfect, and her ruby red dress clung to her in a way that made it hard for Todd to concentrate. His hands itched with the need to touch her.

I can't keep denying the way I feel, Todd admitted to himself. Dana was way more than just a friend to him. At least, he wanted her to be way more than just a friend. But they'd both been burned so badly before. Would they just end up burning each other?

Todd recalled how Dana's hazel eyes had sparkled as she'd talked about the concert. She was so charming, so vibrant and alive. Wouldn't it be worth risking a little pain just to get closer to someone that exciting?

"So." Todd cleared his throat. "Nice night, huh? Look, you can see the Big Dipper." He pointed out the constellation.

Dana tilted back her head to get a better view. The swanlike, ivory column of her neck looked unbearably sexy, and his breath caught in his throat.

"Something wrong?" Dana turned to him. Her spun-silk shawl slipped from her arms.

Instinctively Todd reached to help her. The feel of her bare skin was intoxicating, and her silken hair brushed his fingers as he adjusted the shawl about her shoulders. "Nothing's wrong," he said huskily.

"Thank you." Dana stared at him for a second. Her face was inches from his, and her crimson lips were parted slightly.

Come on, Todd urged himself. *Take a chance! All you have to do is move one inch closer and you'll be kissing.*

Todd stepped forward uncertainly. As he did so, Dana teetered on her high heels.

"Oops!" She grabbed Todd's arm, sending shivers running through his entire body. But when he helped her steady herself, her face was no longer within kissing range. Todd felt simultaneously relieved and disappointed.

"Well, here we are," Todd said as they neared the deserted bus stop. He considered reaching for Dana, but he shoved his hands in his pockets before he could make a fool of himself.

"Thanks for a great evening," Dana said softly. "I had a wonderful time, but you don't have to wait with me. . . . It's perfectly safe."

"I *want* to wait with you, Dana. I don't want the evening to . . . uh, what I mean is, of *course* I'll wait with you."

"Thank you," Dana said simply.

Todd nodded, aware that Dana probably couldn't see the look in his eyes in the darkness, but still he was at a loss for words. He sighed. Why, when the evening had been so fantastic, were things becoming so awkward now?

He had to stop being so scared of getting involved. He really wanted to enjoy being with a woman again. It would be so easy to just take Dana in his arms.

Todd looked at Dana closely. A gentle breeze was stirring her hair, and he could catch the scent of her flowery perfume in the air. Everything was perfect. *Everything*, thought Todd, *except me*.

"Wanna dance, handsome?"

Tom reeled at the scent of beer on the redhead's breath as she pressed herself against him, spilling part of her drink on his clean shirt.

"No, thanks . . . I think I'll sit this one out." Tom's voice was heavy with irony as he tried to disengage himself. It was harder than he would have thought. The redhead seemed to have turned into an octopus, complete with eight slippery arms.

"Wassamatter, handsome? You don't like me?" The redhead planted a sloppy kiss on his cheek.

No, Tom thought, but he merely smiled as he pried himself loose from her grasp and sought refuge on the other side of the room. Boy, was this ever a bad idea. Tom sat down on a seat-sprung couch that gouged his back mercilessly. Between the springs and the two-ton lug who was sprawled out on his left, Tom figured that a bed of nails would have been more comfortable.

"Whatever made me think that a frat party would cheer me up?" he asked himself unhappily. He rubbed his temples in a desperate attempt to soothe the throbbing migraine that was developing in response to the insistent beat of the music.

"Hey, baby, want something?" A blonde in a red minidress leaned close to Tom and whispered in his ear.

What, am I some kind of freak magnet? Tom wondered. "Sorry, no." The blonde pouted and fluttered her eyelashes at him.

"Then how 'bout we dance?" She ran her fingers playfully up and down his hand.

Tom sighed. He knew that most guys would jump at the chance to dance with a woman who looked like this one. But then again, most guys hadn't had the privilege of dating Elizabeth Wakefield. Tom looked around the room. It was packed with women. Beautiful, exciting, fascinating women. There was just one problem. None of them was Elizabeth.

Maybe I should have that drink after all. . . .

Tom shook his head in dismay.

In fact, maybe I should get totally wasted!

No. Tom had no desire whatsoever to wake up with a hangover. As far as he was concerned, his drinking days belonged to the far distant past, when, as Wildman Watts, he'd been able to practically down a keg a night and still keep on his feet. But still, if he couldn't stop thinking about Elizabeth, he was going to have to do something drastic. And right now, a drink looked like a pretty good place to start.

"Excuse me." Tom shifted the blonde, who was trying to make a permanent home on his lap, onto the guy sitting next to him. Both seemed perfectly happy with the arrangement. He elbowed his way through the crowd to the bar. He reached into the barrel of ice-cold drinks that stood off in the corner and cracked open two cans of beer.

"Hey, bro." A bleary-eyed frat boy clapped him on the back. "I know how you feel. Why wait for seconds when you can have them right away!" He weaved back and forth uneasily before sliding to the floor.

Tom tilted back his head and let the frosty brew slide down his throat.

"That's better." He wiped his mouth on his sleeve and caught sight of Danny dancing on the other side of the room. At least, he *thought* it was Danny. Tom squinted through the haze of smoke. He was sure he could make out the striped sweater that Danny had been wearing, but when was the last time he'd seen his roommate dance like that?

Danny flailed around wildly, careening off walls, a goofy grin on his face. Correction—a *drunken* grin. Tom winced when he saw Danny bump into a couple and nearly go sprawling on the floor.

Tom dumped his beers in a planter that seemed to have alternative life-forms growing in it and went to rescue his friend. "Hey, Danny, maybe it's time to lay off the booze." Tom removed the drink from Danny's hand.

"But Tom," Danny protested. "Let us drink and be merry, for who knows what tomorrow will bring?"

"I don't know about tomorrow, but right now is going to bring some fresh air." Tom grabbed Danny's sweater and propelled him out of the room. "Come back in after a few lungfuls," he called good-naturedly over his shoulder as he returned to the party.

Maybe I should just get out of here, Tom thought as he stood on the threshold of the noisy room. He was hardly having "a great time." He needed to help Danny get home, clearly. And he couldn't stop thinking about Elizabeth. He kept thinking he was seeing her everywhere. On the front porch, in the kitchen, on the arm of a guy who was built like a Mack truck—

"Wait a minute," Tom spluttered. "That *is* Elizabeth. *My* Elizabeth. And she's dating the missing link." Glowering, his hands bunched into fists at his sides, Tom made his way across the dance floor.

"Hey, babe, I need a refill. You want one?" The big, blond musclehead twirled Elizabeth in his arms and spun to a stop near the bar.

"No, thanks." Elizabeth smiled at her partner through clenched teeth. If there was one thing she hated, it was being called babe. She adjusted the strap of her dress where it had fallen down her arm and stepped back slightly to disengage herself from his arms.

"Catch you later, then." The musclehead grinned affably and squeezed Elizabeth's shoulder before plunging into the crowd in search of refreshments.

Elizabeth shifted uncomfortably back and forth on her high heels. The charm of the party was starting to wear thin. At first it had been fun to behave in a totally un-Elizabeth-like way and dance with a million different guys, but after a couple of hours she realized there was a very good reason why she didn't often go to frat parties.

They're loud, smoky, and obnoxious . . . and those are just the good things, she thought with a sarcastic laugh as she scanned the crowd for Nina. She felt like leaving, and she hoped that she could convince her friend to do the same.

Elizabeth stood on her tiptoes to look over the heads of several large basketball players. "Where's Nina?" she murmured. She didn't want to leave without her. There was Denise, and Winston, and Tom . . . Tom! "I don't believe it!" Elizabeth muttered angrily.

Tom was staring right at her, and from the look on his face he was none too pleased to see her. If he looked any angrier, smoke would be coming out of his ears. Elizabeth wrapped her arms around herself and prepared to stare him down. What had *he* got to look so mad about anyway? She hadn't done anything to make him jealous . . . yet.

A sly smile spread across Elizabeth's face as she looked around. Preppy frat boys, awesomely built football players, and handsome foreign-exchange students surrounded her. *Mmm, looks like I'm spoiled for choice,* Elizabeth thought, giggling mischievously. She tapped a tall, blond football player on one of his massive shoulders. She'd grown tired of dark men, she decided.

The guy turned around, and she gasped. He was an Adonis.

Elizabeth smiled at him flirtatiously and batted her eyelashes. A slow jam started to play. "Do you want to dance?" she asked coyly, aware that Tom's eyes were on her.

"I thought you'd never ask." He took her in

his arms, and they swayed together in time with the music.

Elizabeth sighed and entwined her arms around Blond Adonis's neck. She'd forgotten how good it felt to be in a man's arms. His dazzling blue eyes stared wordlessly into hers, and she found herself getting lost in them.

Elizabeth tilted back her head and smiled seductively. It was all the invitation the guy needed. She closed her eyes and sighed with pleasure as his mouth crushed against hers.

Kiss me, kiss me . . . please. Dana concentrated on sending Todd her thoughts. *Read my mind, Todd,* she begged silently. Every fiber of her being cried out to be held within the circle of his strong arms.

For the first part of the evening, Dana had to keep reminding herself that they weren't *really* on a date. But as they'd relaxed over pastries and cappuccinos, Dana had to admit the truth to herself: She *was* on a date. A date with a man she was rapidly falling for.

Dana looked over at Todd as he stood motionless in the moonlight. He seemed somewhat tense, with his hands jammed into his pockets. *Did something go wrong?* she wondered.

Still, if Todd seemed tense, he sure made it look good. His dark hair shone in the moonlight, and his face took on a chiseled quality. Dana wondered what his skin felt like. Was it perfectly smooth? She thought that she could see a hint of manly stubble, but it was clear that he'd shaved before meeting her—she could smell the spicy aftershave that he wore as it floated toward her on the breeze.

With a small frown Dana glanced at the delicate evening watch she wore. The bus was due any minute. Todd *had* to do something soon. If not, she was going to have to make the first move.

Do I dare tell him how I feel? Dana asked herself. *What if he doesn't feel the same way?* Dana had always prided herself on being able to gauge the kind of effect she was having on a man, but now she felt strangely vulnerable.

"Todd?" she began tentatively.

"Yeah?" Todd's gaze was so intense that Dana forgot what she was going to say.

"I, um, never mind."

"OK." Todd nodded affably.

Dana sighed in disappointment. She could see the bus as it turned a corner a few blocks away, and her stomach did a small somersault.

Dana took a deep breath. "I just wanted to say . . . what a great time I had," she finished lamely. The bus stopped at a red light.

"Me too," Todd said.

So much for that! Dana watched as the light changed and the bus barreled toward them. She knew she had only a few seconds left, but she was at a complete loss. Dana fiddled uselessly with her evening bag. *Maybe I should . . .* But before she could finish the thought, the bus was in front of her.

The doors opened with a whoosh. Dana swallowed her disappointment and prepared to board. She placed her foot on the first step. But then something told her to stop. Impulsively Dana spun around. Before she could say a word, she was scooped up into Todd's arms, and he kissed her as if he never wanted to breathe again.

Tom felt as if he had been kicked in the stomach as he stood helplessly by and watched Elizabeth allow herself to be pawed by a guy who looked as if he were built out of concrete. She looked as if she was enjoying every last second of that Neanderthal's attention. Tom's brow gathered in an angry frown as he watched Elizabeth practically *purr* with delight.

"I can't take this," Tom muttered angrily. If she thought that he was going to stand idly by and watch her make a spectacle of herself, she had another thing coming. He rolled up his sleeves and cracked his knuckles. Wildman Watts was about to put in a command performance.

He crossed the room in three long strides and tapped Elizabeth's suitor on the shoulder.

"Anything I can do for you?" The guy wiped some of Elizabeth's lipstick off his mouth.

"Yeah." Tom balled his hands into fists. "Stand still for a second." Tom wound up and socked the guy on the jaw.

Yow! Tom resisted the urge to grab his hand in pain and hop up and down on one foot. Clearly the guy's jaw had been chiseled out of granite. The missing link stared at him in a none-too-friendly fashion, and Elizabeth watched the whole thing as if she couldn't care less.

Why is he looking at me like that? Tom wondered as he massaged his hand. The guy clearly didn't have anything to be mad about. Tom's punch barely dented his jaw.

Out of the corner of his eye Tom saw Danny come back inside and begin to make his way over. Tom was also aware that the room had fallen silent and that everyone was watching him. But he didn't care. He was too busy watching the blond giant roll up his sleeves.

"Got a problem, buddy?" The two-ton lug put out his hand to tap Tom on the shoulder. Tom went sprawling as if he had just been hit by a ton of bricks. His face flushed tomato red as he looked up into the amused face of Elizabeth Wakefield.

This was *not* what Tom had planned.

"You with this loser?" The missing link jerked his thumb in Tom's direction.

Elizabeth shook her head wordlessly and allowed the victor to lead her away into the crowd.

"Hey, Tombo." Danny crouched beside him. "Looks like it's my turn to get you out of here." He helped Tom to his feet. "C'mon, I think we've both had enough of this party."

As Tom staggered through the room, the crowd parted for him like the Red Sea. No one would meet his eyes, and worst of all, as he made his way out the door, he was sure that he could hear Elizabeth's tinkling laugh growing louder and louder behind him.

Jessica lay flat on her back as the tears streamed ceaselessly from her eyes. She was alone, with only a teddy bear that Nick had won for her at a fair for company. Elizabeth was at the Alpha Delt party, along with most of the rest of the floor, and the dorm was eerily silent. The only noise that echoed through the walls of room 28, Dickenson Hall, was the sound of Jessica's sobs.

She swiped at her tears with the teddy bear's paw and reached under her pillow for a manila envelope that was stuffed to overflowing with pictures of Nick. Jessica shook the envelope out on the floor. She slid off the bed and knelt down among the pictures with the teddy still firmly clutched at her side.

"This is when we went to the beach, Nick." Jessica picked up one of the photos and studied it closely. She chewed her cuticles relentlessly as she drank in the details of his face. "You have the greenest eyes—did I ever tell you that?" She couldn't remember if she ever had. Oh, sure, Nick had been in no doubt that she thought he was gorgeous, but had she ever come right out and told him how much she loved his eyes? All of a sudden the question seemed overwhelmingly important. "I hope I told you, Nick," Jessica whispered. "I hope I told you because I never will be able to now."

Jessica laid the picture down as if it were as fragile as glass and picked up another one. In it Nick was wearing a leather jacket and staring into the camera with an unbearably sexy half smile on his face. He looked like James Dean.

"Now, I *know* I told you that, Nick." Jessica rocked back and forth, holding the picture against her heart. "I know I told you because you laughed at me and said that I must be in love to think something that crazy. But Nick"— Jessica kissed the photo tenderly—"you looked better than James Dean."

Jessica scooped up a handful of photos. There was one of Nick taken unawares outside the police station, talking to Dub. In another he was behind the wheel of his Camaro, drinking a soda. One shot was of him and Jessica together, running on the beach. Somehow Jessica had managed to catch a complete portfolio of Nick's life on film. There was the sexy Nick, the serious Nick, the hardworking Nick, and the carefree Nick. Each shot captured a different aspect of him, yet they all had one thing in common.

He was alive.

"You were alive, Nick," Jessica whispered, her heart ripping in two as she let the photos fall through her fingers. "But now you're dead, and I'm alone."

Jessica stared blankly at the walls as the pictures tumbled around her. She got up and, dragging her teddy bear by the paw, trampled over the glossy snapshots as if they were no longer sacred to her. "They don't matter," Jessica cried. "They don't matter because nothing matters. Nick is dead, and so am I." She clambered back onto her bed and buried herself in her purple satin comforter, hugging the bear close to her.

"But I'm not dead," Jessica wept. "Because if I were dead, I'd be with Nick now. If I were dead, I'd be happy." Her tears dripped down onto the bear's golden fur. "I'm only dead inside."

She hugged the teddy bear hard, harder. Her shoulders shook with silent sobs. "I can't make it without you, Nick. I can't go on," she gasped. "The world is too hard without you."

Jessica thought of all the things that had once filled her life. She'd loved her friends and been loved in return, she'd loved being a college student, she'd loved the whirlwind of activities she faced every day, but most of all, she'd loved Nick.

But all that ended in the courtroom when the shot rang out. One small ball of lead that sped through the air at over a thousand miles an hour had been enough to change things forever.

"I'll never see Nick again. I'll never love anyone again," Jessica moaned. "I'm alone now, I'll be alone tomorrow, and I'll be alone next week. I'll never feel good again." Jessica held her teddy bear at arm's length and looked him in the eye.

"You know what I think, Teddy?" she choked out between sobs. "I think that I'm not going to make it. Everyone thinks that I'm a survivor. Did you know that about me? Nick did. But I'll tell you something." Jessica held up a finger for emphasis. "I'm not going to make it through this one." Jessica shook her head stubbornly.

"I'm not going to make it through this one,"

she repeated. "Jessica Wakefield is checking out."
The teddy bear dropped from her hand, and the
tears continued to fall. Jessica wasn't just mourning Nick's death. She was mourning her own life.

He adjusted the focus on his infrared military-
grade binoculars to get a better view of her as she
lay sprawled on her bed, the teddy bear dangling
by her side.

The lenses followed the path of a single tear
as it slowly made its way down her cheek.

The binoculars jerked back suddenly. Jessica
had looked straight at him, as if she had known
she was under surveillance.

Does she know? he wondered, lowering the
binoculars. Even more important than tracking
Jessica Wakefield's movements was the need for
absolute secrecy.

With a deep sigh he threw down the binoculars and buried his head in his hands. *Sleep. I
need sleep.* Round-the-clock surveillance was an
exhausting job.

But he could always sleep later. Watching
Jessica was his assignment, and it needed to be
fulfilled. The gloved hand picked up the binoculars again and reset the focus.

Jessica was talking to herself. Lip-reading had
been an essential part of his training, and it was
possible to make out what she was saying.

"I'm alone now," she wept as she rocked back and forth. "I'm alone now."

No, Jessica, you're not alone, the man thought, a smile cutting across his face. *You'll never be alone. Not when I'm here, watching your every move. . . .*

Can a man from Jessica's past help her on the road to recovery? Or will he just drive her closer to self-destruction? Find out in Sweet Valley University #46, I'LL NEVER LOVE AGAIN.

senioryear

SVH

—you've **NEVER** been here before . . .

Available January 1999 wherever books are sold.

The *ONLY* Official Book on Today's Hottest Band!

0-440-41636-1

Get up close and personal with Justin, J.C., Lance, Chris, and Joey as they discuss—in their own words—their music, their friendships on and offstage, their fans, and much more!

On sale now wherever books are sold.

And don't miss

Available wherever music and videos are sold.

Dell
BFYR 215A